"I really need to t
said. **"I have no memory of last night.**

"The last thing I remember is calling you. I did call you, didn't I?"

"You did." Lindy could safely admit that much.

"I really must have done a good one last night," Shane went on. "My grandfather stopped by this afternoon, and pointed out that I have a hickey. Boy, did I get a lecture."

Lindy's hand flew up to cover her mouth. She'd been so carried away last night that she hadn't stopped kissing him. But the evidence was right there in front of her like a badge of honor on Shane's neck.

Shane frowned. "Lindy, how did I get this? I remember a redhead, but I know I didn't do anything with her. But if I have this, who was I with?"

Lindy's heart constricted. At the moment he looked so vulnerable. Yet she knew she couldn't tell him the truth. How could she just say, *Shane, you slept with me.* He always saw her as good old Lindy, his personal assistant.

She gave Shane a narrow look, and he turned his big blue puppy-dog eyes on her. "Let me guess. You want me to find out...."

Dear Reader,

Love often finds people when they least expect it. And often when true love does come, it's not what the person envisioned love to be. Since it isn't what it should look like, it must not be love. Right? Shane Jacobsen has a misguided vision of love. It's right under his nose, but unfortunately he's never seen Lindy Brinks as anything more than the best personal assistant he's ever had. To Shane, love is a fairy tale, a myth. He's also stubbornly set in his ways.

Lindy Brinks knows there's more depth to Shane Jacobsen than most people see. Tired of loving him, though, she's determined to get over Shane once and for all. She's going to get a new job and a new life. Unfortunately, there's a little matter of what she did "last night" that may complicate things....

One of my greatest joys as a published author is creating interesting characters. I also enjoy writing about their evolution and growth as they travel down the rocky path toward true love. When they find it, that love may not be what they expected, but it's better. It's exactly what they need to be happy for the rest of their days. I hope you enjoy Shane and Lindy's story as much as I did writing it. Oh, and about last night...well, you'll just have to read on to see.

Enjoy the romance!

Michele Dunaway

Books by Michele Dunaway

HARLEQUIN AMERICAN ROMANCE

ABOUT LAST NIGHT...
Michele Dunaway

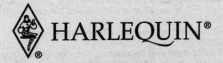

HARLEQUIN®

TORONTO • NEW YORK • LONDON
AMSTERDAM • PARIS • SYDNEY • HAMBURG
STOCKHOLM • ATHENS • TOKYO • MILAN • MADRID
PRAGUE • WARSAW • BUDAPEST • AUCKLAND

ISBN 0-373-75012-9

ABOUT LAST NIGHT…

Copyright © 2004 by Michele Dunaway.

This edition published by arrangement with Harlequin Books S.A.

Visit us at www.eHarlequin.com

Printed in U.S.A.

For Jon Bizzell, who knows why.
To John Eagan, author unknown—believe.
To my Alpha Xi Delta sisters, for always being there.
And to my Pike buddies Alan, Ronn and Kevin,
this one's for you.

ACKNOWLEDGMENT:

Special thanks to Dr. Braxton DeGarmo
for his expertise regarding emergency-room medicine
and head injuries. Any errors in the work are mine.

Prologue

Jacobsen Enterprises External E-mail
From: Joe Jacobsen, CEO, jjacobsen
jacobsen.com
To: Shane Jacobsen, sjacobsen
hmail.com
CC: Blake Jacobsen, bjacobsen
jacobsenministries.com
Date: Friday, April 13
Subject: Job

Shane,

Happy birthday, Grandson!

Now that you are twenty-five, I'm going to ask you once again to join the family company. I've attached a job description that I hope will finally tempt you. I'll stop by your place Saturday to discuss it with you.

P.S. Your grandmother and I expect to see you at our estate this Sunday for Easter dinner. Be there at five and feel free to bring that lovely assistant of yours, Lindy. If you have questions, don't hesitate to contact me.

J.J.

Chapter One

It had been the best, and worst, sex of her life. As Lindy Brinks sat up in bed, she wondered how she could have done it.

Wait.

She knew how. If she hadn't learned that poignant lesson the *first* time, the man still sleeping beside her had made the second and third lovemaking experiences even more satisfying and more invigorating. His chiseled body had been hard and muscular under her fingers, smooth to her touch, and darn if she hadn't been swept away all night long.

No, the real question wasn't what she'd done or how she'd done it, but rather why. For in making love with Shane Jacobsen, Lindy had just made the worst mistake of her twenty-eight-year-old life.

Shane Jacobsen was infuriating. Mind-blowing. Condescending. Phenomenal. A womanizer. Her boss.

And she'd made love to him with her brown eyes wide open, her five-foot-seven body more than willing. Oh yes, definitely more than willing.

As Lindy looked around Shane's bedroom, she

knew she had no one to blame but herself. No one had forced down her throat the strawberry daiquiris she'd drunk last night during Shane's twenty-fifth birthday celebration-slash-pool party. After Shane handed her the first red slushy concoction, Lindy had made the subsequent trips to the bar herself. She really had no excuse for her wanton behavior.

Grimacing, Lindy climbed out of bed, careful not to wake him. She tripped over something soft, and as she caught herself against the bed, she saw Shane's comforter beneath her feet. That had been tossed aside early in the evening. Lindy cringed as she stepped over it. Shane Jacobsen was a playboy to the nth degree, so why had she let herself join his long line of female conquests? Being Shane's personal assistant, she knew every single detail of what he was all about.

Fool! Fool! Fool!

Mentally cursing herself, Lindy slipped into her undergarments and touched her hair. The back of her head felt like a rat's nest and she tugged, desperately trying to use her fingers to straighten the blond strands snarled by the pleasures of the night before. The morning-after movement sent a sharp, searing pain between her eyes, reminding Lindy again exactly how much alcohol and how little sleep she'd had. Fixing her hair without a brush was hopeless.

A small groan escaped Shane, and distracted by the sound, Lindy took a moment to study the man sleeping on the rumpled sheets. For three years now she'd worked for him, watching women practically throw themselves at him, including the buxom redhead who had been nibbling on his ear when Lindy had arrived at last night's party. And despite herself and her desire to do otherwise, she couldn't blame all those women for falling for Shane. There was no denying that he was beautiful.

His straight, naturally surfer-blond hair fell forward into his face, and Lindy resisted the urge to sweep it back from his high cheekbones and chiseled nose. No, last night she'd already had her hands in those strands way too much. She'd committed enough mistakes for one evening, and she certainly didn't need to start over now that the sun was up.

But wasn't that one of life's little ironies? She hadn't planned on staying at his party, especially after she'd realized that Shane, who never drank, had had several of the daiquiris himself.

Lindy remembered cringing, knowing that Shane had been on some pretty impressive painkillers after wrenching his knee during a basketball game the Wednesday night before. No wonder he'd been having such a good time at his party. The label, the one he'd obviously ignored, had said not to mix the medicine with alcohol.

But that was typical Shane. A typical male, he thought he was invincible. And being his personal assistant, aka keeper, she'd stayed, especially after he'd detached himself from the redhead, come over to her side and shouted, "Everyone, this is Lindy, the love of my life. Lindy, everyone."

It had been like something from a classic John Hughes teenage-angst movie. "Hey, Lindy," various faceless people had shouted, and then Shane had pressed a frozen strawberry daiquiri into her hand.

''Come on, Lindy. Let's have fun,'' he'd said, and then he'd swept her along, never quite allowing her to leave his side. So when he'd turned to her later that night, telling her that he needed a birthday kiss, she'd given him just one.

But then his seeking lips had demanded another, and then another.

And Lindy, freed by the alcohol she usually avoided like the plague, had let him lead her right down the path of temptation and eternal destruction. And kissing him—no, she didn't need to think about how wonderful that had been or how good his lips had felt.

She watched Shane nestle deeper into the fluffy down pillow. Thankfully his eyes were closed. Like all his siblings and cousins, Shane had inherited the Jacobsen blue eyes—light blue with an outer darker rim. The promise of wickedness and pleasures evident in his gorgeous eyes had been her absolute undoing last night.

Lindy turned away and started searching for the rest of her clothes. Embarrassment stole over her as she discovered various pieces, including her jeans, in the living room.

Finally dressed, she stood in the doorway to Shane's bedroom and allowed herself one last look. The white sheet had slipped to his waist, revealing the well-muscled chest she had palmed with wild abandon. Lindy resisted the urge to go and cover his nakedness with the sheet. Best she never get that close to him again.

She slipped on her flats and walked stealthily to the pool-house door. Moving out was something his grandfather had been hounding him about of late. But why should Shane move when he commandeered, rent-free, the entire two-thousand-square-foot pool house that sat on his father's estate?

Besides, it wasn't as if Shane ever saw his world-famous parents. This month they were somewhere in Australia doing charity work and evangelical revivals. With a ministry second only to the Billy Graham dynasty, Blake and Sara Jacobsen were usually quite embarrassed about their wayward, playboy son.

That was when they remembered him at all, which was why their son had thrown the impromptu party. Lindy sighed as she reached for the door handle. She couldn't blame her mistake on Blake and Sara Jacobsen's forgetfulness. Even if Shane had been raised mainly by nannies, and he stayed close to home just to be a thorn in his parents' sides, sleeping with him was no one's fault but her own.

As Lindy turned the doorknob, she took one last look at the living area. Shane's shorts lay near the coffee table and empty beer bottles were everywhere. Had Shane had beer, too? Even though he had the reputation of a playboy, in her three years of working for him, Lindy had never seen him liquored up like last night. She shook her head to clear it, wincing as the pain hit her forehead again.

The writing was on the wall. *Fool,* she cursed herself again as she pulled the door shut behind her. Time to find another job.

SHANE JACOBSEN STRETCHED, and then let his head fall back onto the soft down pillow. Darn, did his head hurt.

He blinked. The bright sunlight that was filtering in the blinds hurt his eyes worse than the chlorine in the pool. Tossing his arm over his forehead, he shaded his face from the harsh whiteness illuminating his room. Just what time was it anyway? Eight? No one should be up this early on a Saturday morning.

Or was it Sunday? He moved his arm and faced reality as he realized that, much to his surprise, he really didn't know. His last vague memory was of burrowing his face into something soft, probably his pillow. He sat up, his head pounding from the movement as he tried to remember. Friday he'd turned twenty-five, and the entire event was one long blur.

He felt so over the hill.

He stumbled to the ensuite bathroom, his feet tripping over the cowboy boots he'd left on the floor. He stared at them for a moment. Why were those still there? Why hadn't Cleo come in to clean yet?

Oh, yeah. Now he remembered. Cleo was off for the weekend because it was Easter. That was probably the excuse his father would use when he finally remembered to call. Despite himself, Shane wanted to laugh again at the bitter irony of it all. Good Friday and Friday, April 13, Shane's birthday and that of his father, had been on the same day.

When Shane had realized he'd been forgotten—again—he'd decided to throw himself one hell of a party. Or at least he thought he had. Odd, that the memory of the evening was totally black and blank.

Shane frowned as he finished his business and brushed his teeth. There was something about minty-fresh breath that made him feel at least a little better. Then, and only then, did he dare face himself.

Well, Shane old buddy, he said to his reflection in the mirror, welcome to your late twenties. You look like hell.

He did too. His blond hair was well tousled, as if he hadn't gotten a lot of sleep last night. Stubble covered his jaw, and the Jacobsen-blue-colored eyes that the grandchildren all shared were bloodshot. And was that a red spot on his neck? He rubbed it and shrugged when it didn't disappear.

He could do with a tall glass of ice water.

The clear icy liquid, though, did little to clear his throbbing head or make his blank memory come back. He winced, suddenly unable to erase the feeling that something, although he didn't know what, had happened to him besides drinking while taking medication. Like many people, he'd ignored the warning labels. After all, weren't the labels really only there so people didn't sue the drug companies? You know, sort of like expiration dates that were never quite right?

Maybe one really did feel older when one turned twenty-five. Shane blinked and stared at the red display of the clock in the built-in microwave. Three-twenty-nine. It was after three in the afternoon?

He ran a hand against the stubble that had started to itch. He never slept this late. Man, okay, he'd learned his lesson. He'd follow the labels from now on.

Still clutching the glass of water, he wandered into the living room. He frowned. Odd. Why were his shorts there? He glanced down at the boxers he'd pulled on when he'd gotten up. No surprise there. He always slept naked. But his shorts?

Maybe he'd gone swimming. Vaguely he remembered that others had, enjoying the pool that his parents always opened early and kept perfectly heated until the St. Louis weather warmed fully, usually by the end of May. But taking a swim didn't sound right. So exactly what had he done? Had he been with someone? He remembered a redhead trying at one point to nibble on him, but no, he knew without a doubt he hadn't gotten together with her in any way.

But something was missing and he wished he could remember what it was. He sat down on the couch and surveyed the room. Cleo was going to have a fit when she saw the mess. He pushed aside someone's half-empty bottle of beer so that he could put his feet up.

"Quite a mess you have here."

Shane inwardly groaned as his paternal grandfather stepped through the front entryway. Despite his grandfather's appearance of a thinner version of Santa Claus, Shane knew this visit would be far from jolly. "Feel free to come on in."

"Seeing that the door was open, I already did. Celebrated a quarter of a century with a bang, didn't you?" Grandpa Joe said. Shane knew what his grandfather saw: beer bottles and empty daiquiri glasses everywhere. Plates of partially eaten food littered end tables. The living room was a mess.

Grandpa Joe rubbed his snow-white beard thoughtfully before he said, "I take it your father forgot to call. He always was terrible about dates, including his own birthday. Some secretary must have dropped the ball on this one."

Shane avoided the truth. "Marci and Dan suggested the party. Why not? I turned twenty-five. My car insurance drops now."

Grandpa Joe's Jacobsen-blue eyes blinked once as he let Shane's statements slide. "Of course you should celebrate. You've reached a milestone. Which is why I'm here. I have a business proposition for you."

The dull ache between Shane's eyebrows intensified. He rubbed the spot. Not again. He knew his grandfather meant well, but didn't everyone realize that no meant no? "Grandpa Joe, don't bother. You know the answer is no. I'm not coming to work for Jacobsen."

Grandpa Joe took a few steps toward the couch; then, seeing an additional mess, decided against sitting down. "Shane, it's past time for you to take your destiny. I have the perfect position for you."

"I've told you before—I don't want a position. I have no desire to work for Jacobsen Enterprises. Ever."

Grandpa Joe made the rare gesture of tossing his

hands. "You are so frustrating! You won't even listen. What is it with you? You weren't diagnosed as oppositional defiant as a child. Why is it that every time someone suggests something, you dig in like a stubborn old Missouri mule? Is it the only way you can get the attention your parents always forgot to give you as you grew up? Hell, you'd stay in a burning building if someone from the family tried to pull you out. We are not your enemy, Shane."

Shane clasped his hands together to remain calm. His parents and his family were not the issue, and if they were, he didn't want to think about it or how many times either his parents or his grandparents had told him they were disappointed in him for not following the path they'd laid out. "I try to keep business and family separate."

"That's impossible. We have a family business. You are family. You are needed in the business. You have a business degree and you are darn good. One of the finest I've seen. Doesn't that matter?"

"Look, this isn't a good time. I've got to clean up this mess and call Lindy and…" Shane's voice drifted off as he realized Grandpa Joe was staring at him. "What?"

"Is that a hickey on your neck?"

Shane rubbed at the spot he'd seen in the mirror earlier. It was a hickey? He hadn't had one of those since ninth grade. And if he had a hickey, who had he been with?

"Shane, look, I know your father made some mistakes with you. He and your mother either spoiled you rotten or put you out of their minds and let overindulgent nannies raise you while they went out and saved the world. Perhaps I was wrong to not have stepped in earlier and done something about it when you were younger. But you're twenty-five now. You need to accept your responsibilities to this family instead of languishing like some pathetic playboy with no purpose. If you won't think of yourself, at least think of Lindy."

Shane bristled. "Leave Lindy out of this."

"No, I won't. The girl has raw business talent. She's wasted working for you. What do you do that requires a PA? Does she add legitimacy or something to your endeavors?"

"I do real work. My foundation."

"Yes, your foundation. The one redeeming feature you have. Your foundation is quite generous and you run it well. But that and multiplying your trust fund are not real work." Grandpa Joe paused. "And Lindy is wasted simply stuffing envelopes and getting rid of your exes. Maybe I should steal her away from you."

"Don't you dare go near Lindy. Besides, taking her won't get what you want. I won't come work for you."

Grandpa Joe shook his head. "You know I love you, grandson, but it's not all about you. You've become an empty man, Shane. You skate by because you won't risk. You choose not to face your demons. I can only hope you wake up and realize that fact before it's too late to see what's in front of you. All good things are worth risk. That being said, I'll see you at Easter dinner. Your grandmother would love it if you brought

Lindy. I'll see both of you tomorrow.'' And with that Grandpa Joe stepped over some empty beer bottles and left.

Shane took a long drink of water. He hated being out of control, and Grandpa Joe's visit had left him reeling. Shane wasn't afraid of risk. He just had his reasons for not working at the family company, that was all. Besides, he'd carved out a good life for himself. His stubbornness had nothing to do with growing up with minister parents who were always promoting Christianity, saving lost souls and leaving their son in the capable hands of nannies. He'd turned out fine. He just didn't fit the mold his family created for him.

Enough was enough, Lindy would always tell him. Good old Lindy. She was always there for him, and like always, Shane knew he'd get over this latest dramatic family setback and letdown.

Shane just wished he could remember what had happened. Throwing pity parties wasn't his style. Not only that, but he never drank much, maybe one drink now and then. Last night had been an exception.

He pushed a wayward strand of hair out of his face. Hopefully he hadn't done anything that would tarnish the family name further or he'd be sure to hear about *that.*

Maybe Lindy would know what he'd done, and who besides Marci and Dan had been at the party. Good old Lindy. She was worth more than he paid her. Sure, he knew what everyone whispered. Just as his grandfather had said earlier, everyone agreed. Everyone said he really didn't need a personal assistant; after all, all he truly did was day-trade and run the Shane Jacobsen Foundation that donated to child-abuse agencies. But Lindy was indispensable, as she'd proved over and over again. And right now he needed her. That thought cheered him up. She'd never let him down before, and he knew she wouldn't now. All he had to do was ask and she'd make it her job to find out what happened at his party.

Thankfully the cordless phone was still in its place on the end table. Shane picked it up and pushed a button, the only one besides the pizza place that got any use from the phone's speed dial feature.

"Hello!"

"Lindy! It's me! Can you—" he began.

"I'm sorry, but I'm not available to take your call right now. Please—"

Shane fumed through the rest of her voice mail's message. Odd. Where was Lindy? Why wasn't she answering her cell phone? Even in the dead of night she always answered her cell phone. He tried to remember her pager number as the voice mail beeped the record prompt at him.

"Lindy? Damn it, if you're there call me. I need to ask you about last night. Do you have any clue what happened to me? Except for this pounding headache, I don't remember a darn thing."

AT SIX-THIRTY LINDY TOSSED aside the *St. Louis Post-Dispatch*. The Sunday employment section, available early Saturday afternoon, had held slim pickings. The few jobs that had looked the slightest bit interesting all had a salary far below what Shane paid her. Unless she wanted to take a major pay cut, for a while she was stuck with him.

She glanced at her cell phone. The words announced three missed calls and two new voice-mail messages. "Persistent, isn't he?" She picked up the phone and checked the caller ID display. The first number with multiple calling times was, as she'd thought, Shane's. The second read J. Jacobsen. She frowned. Curious, Lindy dialed her voice mail.

"Lindy, it's Shane. Where are you? I've been calling you all day. I'm starting to get really worried. Call me."

Lindy hit seven-seven, erasing his newest message before his warm baritone washed over her and melted her resolve. As soon as the right job came along, she had to leave him.

The next message was from Shane's grandfather. "Lindy? This is Joe Jacobsen. Would it be possible for you to come to my office Monday at nine? I have a few matters I'd like to discuss with you professionally, and Easter dinner is not the time or place. You do know you're invited? Shane did tell you, right? See you tomorrow and then on Monday."

Lindy erased that message, reached for her day planner and penciled in 9:00 a.m. Joe Jacobsen. She wasn't sure what Shane's grandfather wanted with her on Monday, but in the three years she'd been working for Shane she'd learned to jump when Grandpa Joe said jump. Founder of Jacobsen Enterprises, one of the largest companies in St. Louis, Joe Jacobsen was a self-made man along the lines of Andrew Carnegie. Even though Joe was as kindhearted as a teddy bear, in business and in life he always got what he wanted. As for Easter dinner, she could safely pass on that.

A knock sounded at her door, distracting her from the pressing problem of Shane's faulty memory and the fact that eventually she'd have to call him back. Her pizza had finally arrived. Lindy rose to her feet, glad that she'd taken a shower after her roommate Tina had left. There had been a lecture—all about Shane's shortcomings—that Lindy hadn't needed. She rubbed her head one more time. Her headache had almost totally disappeared, and now with food she'd hopefully finally feel better and find a solution to her current problem.

Besides, after all, she wasn't sure if she was happy, sad or just plain outright furious. Shane Jacobsen had no idea what had happened to him. The best love-making of her life and he didn't remember it. Of course, she'd spent the whole drive home worried about what to say to him. That problem was solved— he didn't remember anything.

But darn him! He wasn't supposed to have blacked out! To be unmemorable, to have been forgotten... She grabbed her checkbook, headed for the door, and pulled it open. Unfortunately, the pizza deliveryman didn't stand on the threshold.

''Shane!''

''There you are!'' Shane rushed in and, before Lindy could move, he enveloped her in a gigantic bear hug. His damp hair fell into his face and an immediate warmth from his body traveled to hers. Her knees wobbled and Shane steadied her before leaning back so that he could see her face. "Lindy, you've had me worried sick. I've been calling you for hours. Why haven't you been answering? You are okay, aren't you?"

Lindy blinked, trying to find focus. Ah, to be in his strong arms again—her traitorous body awakened once more. Her breasts thrust forward as if seeking him, and heat began to pool.

No! Lindy yanked her mind back into full control and drew back a step, away from Shane. Immediate welcome coolness descended as she detached herself from Shane's embrace. Her knees wobbled as she turned her back to him. Control. She needed control. She concentrated on making her step steady as she walked toward the couch. Thankfully he didn't seem to notice.

"Why didn't you call me back?"

"I was taking a nap." Lindy sat down, her legs more secure against the solid green cushions. Then she made the mistake of looking up at him.

Despite looking vexed, to her Shane had never seemed more beautiful. His jeans molded to his athletic legs, and his polo shirt revealed those wonderful arms that had just again held her tight to his chest. And those blue eyes that had held such promise last night right now revealed endless concern and care that was just for her.

How long had she waited for him look at her this way? As if he felt something for her?

Again she wanted to drown in him, to feel him against her, to let the illusions wash over her. She could still almost feel the way his fingers had stroked her skin and…

"Lindy, you never nap."

She blinked, fantasy thankfully shattered with his words. "There's always a first time. That is okay, isn't it? I was tired so I turned off the phone and took a nap."

Shane's full lips turned downward and Lindy fought off a sudden urge and desire to kiss away his frown. "I'm being a cad," Shane announced. "Are you sick? Can I get you anything? A pillow? Aspirin? What can I do to help?"

Lindy sighed. How could she get riled up at him? He'd been so worried about her not calling him back that he'd shown up on her doorstep. At moments like this Shane was at his best. Shane was not all his playboy image portrayed. After working with Shane for three years, Lindy knew a Shane few others did. She'd seen him when he'd made a dying child's wish come true; she'd seen him care about situations others had washed their hands of. She'd seen him sit by his friend Dan's hospital bed during Dan's illness. And here he was, showing up because he'd been worried about her. How could she even think of leaving him?

Her mind wrestled with her heart as a desperate resolve filled her. She fisted her hands together. For her own long-term sanity and future she had to try. She could not let herself be sucked into the easy charm that was—and always would be—Shane Jacobsen. She was his personal assistant. That's all she'd ever be, and it was a cruel illusion to pretend otherwise, to dream he might one day fall in love with her.

Deliberately she made her voice cold. "Thanks for being worried about me. But besides that, why are you here? Is there something you needed?"

"Water would be good," Shane said, totally misinterpreting her chilly undertone. He gave her a smile that could have kept the winter frost from harming the spring tulips. Part of her burned, and she struggled for self-control.

"I'll get you some." Grateful for the diversion, Lindy stood, sidestepped Shane, and moved into the kitchen. Once in the safety of the small, enclosed space, she gripped the edge of the counter and gave herself a mental pep talk. She could do this. In Shane's mind nothing had changed between them. He didn't remember last night. That was a good thing. All the aces were in her hand. She could play them any way she wished.

Shane was still standing when she left the kitchen. She handed him the tall glass of ice water, and as their fingers touched a raw electric spark shot through her, the same type of shock that had jolted through her last night. Last night she rationalized her reaction to Shane's touch as being from drinking alcohol. No such excuse existed now. She jumped back and stared at Shane.

"Static," he said.

"Yes," Lindy replied.

As he finished his sip of water she could almost see

the clear liquid slide down his throat, and she swallowed, too. This man was pure charisma. She just needed to think of him clinically now. That was all.

"Thanks," Shane said as he sat down on the sofa. "I was worried because you always call me back."

He took another long drink before placing the glass on a woven coaster that Tina had brought back from one of her trips to London. "I really need to talk to you. I have no memory of last night. The last thing I remember is calling you. I did call you, didn't I?"

"You did." Lindy could admit that safely. Her legs suddenly unsteady again, she sat down in a chair located perpendicular to the sofa where Shane sat.

"At least I remember that much." Shane raked a hand through his now dry hair. "I must have really done a good one last night. Look at this. My grandfather stopped by this afternoon and said I have a hickey." He moved aside the shirt's collar and showed Lindy the spot on his neck. "Boy, did I get a lecture."

Lindy's hand flew up to cover her open mouth, and for a brief, imperceptible moment she closed her eyes. During their passion, she'd left a mark on his neck. He'd been joined with her, and as he'd swept her along to another crest she'd reached up to kiss him, and...

Her eyes flew open and she jerked her telltale hand away from her mouth and put it in her lap. She'd been so carried away that she hadn't stopped kissing him. The evidence was right there in front of her like a badge of honor on Shane's neck. Horrified at what she'd done, she needed all her mettle to steel her face into neutral.

Shane leaned forward and took Lindy's hand in his. The heat from his touch seared her, and she shifted uncomfortably as her body went into overdrive, once again desiring what it had enjoyed a little more than twelve hours earlier. Would she ever stop wanting him, especially now, after she'd had him? She had to try. She yanked her hand from his.

Shane frowned. "Lindy, how did I get this? I remember a redhead, but I know I didn't do anything with her. But if I have this, then who was I with?"

Lindy's heart constricted. At that moment, he looked so vulnerable. But she knew she couldn't tell him the truth. How could she just say, "Shane, you slept with me. I'm the one you don't remember. The one that left that mark on your neck."

Yeah, right. He always saw her as good old Lindy. His PA. A pal. And what type of relationship would she have with Shane if he knew? Not the one she wanted. Men like Shane Jacobsen didn't marry their PAs. Men like Shane didn't even know what love was. They thought it was an illusion, a holy grail. No, best he never know the truth.

She gave Shane a narrow look, and he turned his big blue puppy-dog eyes on her. "Let me guess. You want me to find out for you."

"Yes," Shane said. "It'll look awkward if I ask around. No one at the party needs to know I can't remember. And if anyone can find out discreetly, you can. Please do me this favor."

All afternoon, Lindy had replayed every detail of the previous night at least a million times. Now she mentally ran through the list of party guests again. No one had seen her get together with Shane.

She took a deep breath, steadying herself for the task ahead, the one that she had to do whether she liked it or not. "No," Lindy said.

"What?" Shane's head rebounded and the W-shaped furrow that appeared between his eyes showed his displeasure.

"No," Lindy repeated. She drew another steadying breath. "Shane, I'm sorry, but this is not in my job description."

His look of disbelief was Cary Grant classic. "You're my personal assistant and you're saying no? You've always handled my personal business before. Isn't this personal business?"

"No. It's purely personal, not business. We may have developed a friendship over the years we've worked together, but you're my boss, Shane. It's time each of us remembered that."

"You've done it before, Lindy. Remember when you got rid of Janine for me? She was almost a stalker until you took care of her."

"Perhaps, but she was interfering with business by showing up at the pool house."

"And how is this different from then?"

"It just is. Look at you. You don't even know what happened to you. That's not my job, Shane, it's yours no matter how awkward. From this point forward I'm not going to be involved in your personal life. Period."

Disappointment etched his beautiful features, and at

that moment Lindy knew she'd spoiled Shane. Long before last night she'd crossed the line between professional and personal. She'd become his confidant, his problem-solver and his sounding board.

But no more. Not after last night. She had to redraw the line. She was tired of the one-way relationship. She gave; he took. And since a two-way relationship was just a pipe dream, it was best if she drew the line in the sand and put their relationship purely on a business level once and for all until she found another job.

Nerves buzzing, Lindy took another deep breath and attempted to control her inner shaking. "And while we're at it, Shane, you need to realize that I'm not planning on being with you forever. I've got career aspirations. I want to use my degree, not just schedule your dates and buy them roses or a trinket when you're bored and toss them aside."

"You can't be serious." Shane's jaw dropped open, his look aghast. "You're the best PA I've ever had. You can't leave me. I need you."

Shane needed her. Lindy wanted to cry at that irony. How she wished this was true. She'd taken Psychology 101 in college. Shane really could do all the work for his foundation himself. No, Shane craved attention, not her. Because of his family situation, he'd grown up wanting someone to dote on him, the way she'd been doing the past three years as his personal assistant. That couldn't be her role any longer. Not after last night.

Lindy forced herself to look at Shane. "I'm the only PA you've ever had and I am serious. You need to handle your personal affairs, even if you don't remember them.''

The jaw she'd planted kisses all over dropped open again. ''You really know how to kick a guy when he's down.'' He winced, as if a headache had returned. ''Happy birthday, Shane. Find out yourself who you did last night. By the way, I'm leaving.''

''You're sounding like a spoiled brat,'' Lindy said.

Shane blinked. ''Only you can take such liberties and call me that.''

''But I'm right.''

He exhaled slowly. ''Yes. You're right I have no excuse except to say that this weekend has me out of sorts. Your news on top of the fact that I have this nagging suspicion that something happened is simply not making for a good day.''

Lindy cringed. She'd been raised to be honest and it went against her grain to tell even a small white lie. But she had no better alternative. In this case, the cliché did not fit. The truth would not set her free.

''Look Shane, maybe nothing happened. Maybe it was a gag. Did you ever think of that? That someone just pinched you really hard on your neck.''

Shane's jaw set and a muscle in his cheek twitched. ''I know you dislike my friends, but none of them are that juvenile.''

She suddenly felt like Kevin Costner's character in *No Way Out*. Hiding herself while in charge of finding herself. ''Shane, besides Marci and Dan, most of the people you associate with are a bunch of freeloaders or women who just want to be Mrs. Shane Jacobsen.

Think about that for a moment. I mean, what do you do that's real? Honestly, some days I don't know why you need a PA. It's not as if the work you do is time-consuming.''

''You sound like my grandfather, who also gave me that lecture earlier today.'' Shane let the acrid comment hang for a moment before adding, ''He also wants you to come to Easter dinner tomorrow night.''

Lindy took a cleansing breath. Because of Grandpa Joe's earlier message, she'd had some time to prepare for this dilemma. ''I can't make it.''

Shane stared at her, that beautiful jaw again slightly open. He snapped it shut before speaking. ''You're killing me, Lindy. I don't need any more bad news or the grief of showing up without you.''

''Shane, I'm your employee. Employees do not go to family Easter dinners.''

''I thought you were my friend.'' Shane sat there a long moment. ''I even shared my personal journals with you. I'd never before let anyone see what I'd written.''

He had shared with her, and early in their work relationship, Lindy, starry-eyed with love, had let herself get too close to Shane. Her stomach churned as she remembered.

In one journal, Shane had written about the pain of losing a girl he'd fallen in love with at camp, the summer between fifth and sixth grade. Their love had been that sweet innocent kind between two shy people who hardly talk, yet somehow they know they are meant for each other. How Shane had looked forward to seeing her the next year, only to discover upon his arrival that she was on the charter bus pulling away. Years later, Shane still remembered the way she'd pressed her hand against the dirty glass as she disappeared forever from his view.

Yes, Shane had shared his journals with Lindy, and that day one thing had become certain to Lindy—she could never compete with what Shane envisioned his perfect love to be. Lindy would never be enough— never be the one.

But she'd stayed at her job, mostly because she hadn't had the courage to stay away, becoming daily too attached, falling too hard for the man she cared way too much for, who could never feel the same way in return. But last night she'd well and truly crossed the line, and it gave her a raw, untapped strength. She hated hurting him with her next words, but in the long run it was for the best that a space be placed between them.

"You don't pay your friends," Lindy pointed out.

Shane shook his head, sending his blond hair falling forward across his eyebrow. "That argument is weak, Lindy. Weak. I can see I made a mistake worrying about you. That's something friends would do."

He stood up, his features etched with frustration as if he'd bitten bitter fruit. Lindy's fingers longed to smooth away the lines her words had caused. She knew she'd sucker punched him.

First his parents had forgotten his birthday, and now she'd effectively killed their friendship. But her one-sided relationship with him had to stop. She'd known him too long and knew he'd never find that elusive woman he wanted. She couldn't keep on loving him and remain sane. She had to let him go, even if it was the hardest thing she'd ever do.

"I'm sorry," she said as Shane put his hand on the doorknob. Even to her own ears her apology sounded lame.

He gave her one last look. "You're a great assistant, Lindy. Even though you don't think I really work for a living, I do have some responsibilities. So, I'll see you Monday morning. You are still planning on showing up, aren't you?"

There it was. The perfect opportunity to get out professionally, even if it meant taking a pay cut. She'd already indicated she was leaving. Now all Lindy had to cement it was say, "but only until I find another job." She opened her mouth, but the words finalizing her break with Shane refused to come.

"Monday morning," Lindy agreed with a nod. She couldn't look him in the eye, and instead stared at the floor.

The door clicked when he shut it behind him. Then—and only then—did Lindy look up. She stared at the door to her apartment. It desperately needed a fresh coat of paint.

"I'm thinking about paint." Tears watered her eyes and rivered their way down to wet her cheeks. The opportunity had presented itself, but she hadn't walked away. Would she ever be able to let Shane Jacobsen out of her life? Fool! Fool! Fool! She again resolved to seriously look for a new job come Monday.

Her home phone rang and Lindy picked it up. "Shane?"

"Is this Lindy Brinks?"

Disappointment mixed with relief. "Speaking."

"I'm calling about your pizza. We've had some oven problems and it's going to be at least another half hour before we can deliver it. We're very sorry for the inconvenience. We'll include a coupon for a free pizza the next time you order. You still want it, right?"

"Sure, send it." She hung up the phone, a dark depression settling over her. Shane was like the pizza. She still wanted him, but it certainly wasn't worth the trouble anymore. Too bad she was still hungry.

Chapter Two

"So where's Lindy?"

"Greetings to you, too," Shane said as he stepped through the front door of his grandfather's massive Ladue manse. "Lindy sends her regrets. She can't make it."

"Why?" Grandpa Joe's eyes narrowed and he stroked his white beard thoughtfully. "With her parents on opposite coasts, she doesn't have any family here. Did she go out of town?"

"Lindy's in town and I don't know why she didn't come," Shane replied. "She said she had other plans. Besides, I'm her employer, not her keeper."

Grandpa Joe's snow-white eyebrows arched. "It sounds like you two have had a spat."

Was that what had happened yesterday? A spat? Shane considered Grandpa Joe's antiquated word. In all honesty, even though he'd been thinking about it nonstop, Shane still didn't know quite what had happened. Even writing in his journal about the weekend's events hadn't given him any perspective.

Lindy, good old Lindy who had never once complained about her job, had suddenly hit him between the eyes with what she would and would not do. She was his employee, she'd declared, not his friend. If she'd remain his employee at all.

That still stung. And yes, he'd had to admit to himself in the past twenty-two hours that perhaps he had taken her for granted, that he'd considered her a friend, a sounding board. Perhaps he'd been wrong to have been so free with his confidences and personal requests. But he and Lindy had worked so well together, and never once had she complained.

Shane shifted his weight and followed his grandfather into the huge great room. The rest of the family had already arrived. "Shane!" His half sister Bethany came over and gave him a quick kiss on his cheek. "How are you? I feel like I haven't seen you in ages."

They probably hadn't talked in ages, Shane thought. Older than him by five years, Bethany, his mother's daughter from her first marriage, was busy with her successful pediatric practice, her own two children, and her husband.

"So did you have a good birthday? Twenty-five now." Bethany shook her head. "I can't believe that in a few months I'll turn thirty and that Olivia and Nick will hit that three-o mark just a few months after me."

Shane glanced around the room, seeing his cousin Harry, his wife Megan, and Bethany's clan. Shane's half brother, his dad's son by his first marriage, though, was strangely absent. "Speaking of, where is Nick?"

"He stayed in Chicago," his half sister Olivia said as she approached. She leaned toward her younger sibling and said conspiratorially, "Word has it that Grandpa Joe isn't too pleased with my twin brother. And Claire's in Aruba on a much-needed vacation so she's forgiven. But Nick's not."

"Ah, then maybe the heat will be off me for once," Shane said.

Olivia's blue eyes twinkled mischievously. "I doubt that. You know how gossip runs in this family. It's all over that you had a pretty good party Friday night. Glad it was you and not me. So tell me, have you recovered?"

"All but my memory," Shane admitted. Thankfully it was a cool night and the turtleneck he wore hid the telltale mark. "I even cleaned up some so that Cleo won't throw a fit."

"A wise move," Olivia said. "Did Sara and Dad ever call?"

"Yeah, this afternoon. Of course it was like 7:00 a.m. Australian time, and of course Monday there."

"Ooh," Olivia said. "Did they even try to give you an excuse?"

"You know. New secretary. It was Easter weekend. That type of thing."

"Cocktail, sir?" James, the family butler and groundskeeper of over twenty years, approached.

"Water is fine," Shane answered. "And how is Cindy?"

"She's fine, sir. I'll tell her you inquired."

"He's so funny," Shane said to Olivia after James had moved away.

"Unlike Dad and Sara, I can't imagine a family event without James and his wife," Olivia replied.

"True." Besides being the family cook, Cindy had also been Shane's first nanny. They were practically family. Of course, Lindy wouldn't agree, Shane thought as he reached for the water James was handing him. She'd say they were employees.

The ringing of a knife tapping a glass interrupted Shane's momentary bitterness. His attention diverted, he turned to see his cousin Harry holding up a champagne glass. "Everyone, before we go into dinner, Megan and I have an announcement to make. In eight months you'll be welcoming the newest addition!"

Shane saw his grandmother Henrietta clasp her hands together and hug her husband. Then she went and hugged both Harry and Megan. "I think we need champagne," Grandpa Joe told James.

"On its way, sir."

"Congratulations," Shane said later to his Aunt Lilly, Harry's mother. His hand still clutched his water instead of the expensive bubbly. Lilly, however, was on her second glass.

"Isn't it wonderful? First Darci, and now Harry. I'm so thrilled. My dad and mom are so thrilled. Look at them." Lilly gestured toward Grandpa Joe and Henrietta. "New great-grandbabies on their way. After all, Bethany's youngest is almost five."

"Ah, but they'll be Sanders babies, not Jacobsens,"

Lilly's husband Andrew said as he entered the conversation.

"Oh please, Andrew. My dad doesn't care about that."

"No, but you know the old coot wants a great-grandbaby with the surname Jacobsen."

Lilly shot her husband a look of mock disgust. "My father is not an old coot."

"I work with him. Yes he is."

Lilly's Jacobsen-blue eyes twinkled. She and Andrew had been married for over thirty-five years, and as president of Jacobsen Enterprises, Andrew was Grandpa Joe's right-hand man. "Okay, I'll admit he is. But maybe these great-grandbabies will keep him so busy that it'll stop him from meddling so much."

Andrew laughed, put his arm around her, and pulled his wife closer to his side. "Nah. I'm sure he'll just turn his attention to your brother's children. What do you think about that, Shane? Even though Claire's the eldest, it's only you and Nick who can pass on the Jacobsen name."

"Huh?" He hadn't been paying attention. Both Lilly and Andrew peered curiously at him.

"You aren't worried that you're next in Grandpa Joe's quest to marry off his grandchildren?" Andrew asked.

Was he next? Grandpa Joe had made no secret of his matchmaking and meddling in Darci's and her brother Harry's lives. So was he next? Shane shook his head. Time to put an end to that idea. "You know I love my grandfather, but if he hasn't been able to get me into the family company, do you really think he can pick my wife? He'll have better luck with Nick, not me.''

Andrew laughed, which didn't sit well with Shane. ''Are you certain? I wouldn't put it past him to start with you.''

Great. ''I won't let my guard down.''

Andrew gave Shane a manly pat on the back and Shane had the feeling Andrew knew something he didn't. ''You do that. Be sure you do that.''

''Dinner,'' James announced.

AT THE END of the main course, Henrietta leaned toward Shane. As always, his grandmother smelled of fresh lavender. ''Isn't it wonderful news about Harry and Megan? This old house has been too long without tiny babies.''

Not knowing how to respond, Shane simply nodded. His grandmother smiled, and then placed her warm left hand over his right one. ''You do know the pressure is going to be on you?''

Not again. ''I'm not getting married.''

Henrietta patted his hand. ''Oh no dear, not that. My husband thinks I don't know anything, but there's a bond between a mother and her son. Do you think Blake doesn't tell me what's going on? I know Joe's been trying to get you to the corporate offices for quite a while. And with Megan's job opening up, he's really going to want you. After all, you went to Princeton like he did.''

Shane set his jaw stubbornly. That had been the one

and only thing he'd ever done that had pleased his grandfather. "Family is family, business is business. I don't want to mix the two."

Henrietta gave him a sympathetic smile. "I know, but your grandfather will never understand that. When he sees what he wants, he goes for it. How do you think he won me all those years ago? Stole me away from Steve Boswell. I didn't think your grandfather could be the one. But somehow he wormed his way into my life and swept me right off my feet. One day I just realized that although he wasn't what I'd expected the dream to look like, he was the one that would make it all come true."

Shane frowned. "Well, I'm not liable to just fall for someone he waves in front of my nose. Love is much more than that." *Isn't it?*

"Of course it is. But love isn't just a feeling. It's also a choice. You young people are much more modern these days, so much so that I think you wait for a moment that never comes. Speaking of not coming, what happened to that nice assistant you have? Lindy? I was so disappointed that she wasn't able to be here tonight. But Joe said he'd ask her why tomorrow."

That caught Shane's attention. "Tomorrow?"

"Yes. I think he's meeting her at 9:00 a.m."

"Really." The honeybaked ham that had been dinner flipped in Shane's stomach.

"Dessert," James said. He placed a coconut cake confection down. Despite the beauty of the dessert, Shane didn't think he could tolerate one bite.

Shane stared down the table to where his grandfather sat deep in conversation with Megan. So Grandpa Joe was meeting Lindy tomorrow. Grandpa Joe's words resounded in Shane's head. *Maybe I should just steal her away from you.*

Was that why Lindy had refused to come tonight? Was that why she'd cut him out as a friend? Was she going to Jacobsen Enterprises without him?

Shane's eyes narrowed. Grandpa Joe was as elusive as an eel when necessary. Shane would just have to wait and ask Lindy tomorrow. After all, she never was very good at hiding things from him.

BY NOON Shane found himself pacing the small confines of the room that served as his and Lindy's office. He'd expected her long before this.

Suddenly he heard the front door. He sat in his chair for a brief moment before rising again. Casual. He needed to act casual. He stepped into the living room just as Lindy shut the front door.

Trying to remain calm, he leaned himself against the doorjamb. And then, his body quickening, he just stared. Lindy wore a suit. While he'd seen her before in professional office clothes, something was different. Just when had she gotten those legs? Legs that seemed to run on forever and disappear underneath that short blue skirt? Wow. He'd always thought her pretty, but now…he'd never reacted to Lindy like this before. He swallowed the lump that formed in his throat. "Forget to call me again?"

Lindy drew herself up. The smile she gave him didn't quite meet her eyes. "I'm sorry. I didn't mean to upset you. I thought I told you that I wouldn't be in until noon.''

It was her cool tone that did it, the truth she didn't reveal, that caused Shane to straighten and walk toward her. Despite her heels adding to her five-foot-seven-inch height, Shane's six-foot frame still towered over her. To hell with being casual. ''So tell me, are those clothes just for my benefit?''

''I thought I'd dress up for once. We always dress so casual,'' Lindy replied. She shifted her weight, and Shane stepped closer to her. Lindy blinked.

''Oh Lindy, be honest. Do you think I wouldn't figure it out?''

''You know?'' Panic covered her face, sending powerful emotions flooding into her big brown eyes.

''Of course I know.''

''I didn't think you'd... I mean, I didn't tell you because—''

''I'm not a fool, Lindy. So tell me, did you enjoy your meeting with my grandfather?''

HIS GRANDFATHER. Lindy wanted to laugh with the irony of it all. She'd been thinking, she'd thought, oh, thank goodness. He still had no memory of Friday night.

Lindy took a calming breath to still her racing heart. ''Yes, I met with your grandfather.''

''And?'' Shane leaned closer.

Lindy sidestepped Shane and put her briefcase on the coffee table. Obviously Cleo had been in to clean already. The place was spotless. She turned back to face Shane. Might as well get it over with. "With Megan's announcing her pregnancy and her decision that she wants to stay at home after the baby, your grandfather plans to do some reshuffling of employees. When the time comes he'll fill Megan's spot with someone from his Jacobsen Stars upper-level-management program, but right now he thought I would be perfect for a midlevel position that is currently open."

"I see." Shane ran a hand through his hair. "Just as I expected. He said as much when he came over here Saturday. You do realize that this is all just a ploy to get me into the company? Steal the assistant so the grandson will follow?"

After working for Shane for three years, Lindy knew the entire family situation. But it didn't matter. "I told you I have career aspirations, Shane. There are a lot of benefits to working for Jacobsen. Not that I don't enjoy working for you, but at least at the broker's office I came into contact with other people."

He frowned. "We get a lot of requests for money from the foundation. You're in contact with people all the time."

"Sure, on the phone. I have no work colleagues that I do things with."

"You have me."

That, of course, was the problem. Lindy took a calming breath. "Besides you."

"Is there something wrong with working in a small office?"

Yes! We made love all night! "No, but it's not enough. Not anymore."

Shane again raked his hand through his blond hair, a sure sign he was agitated. "I don't understand you, Lindy. Everything was fine Friday afternoon and today it's night-and-day different. What the hell is going on? Has your roommate been on your case about me again?" He paused, his blue eyes searching her face. "I can see from your expression that she has."

Adopting a defensive posture, Lindy squared her shoulders. "Tina's only looking after my best interests."

"And you don't think that I am?"

Not in the way she needed. But she couldn't tell him that. Thus, for a moment Lindy paused, remembering the conversation she and Tina had had. Tina had called Shane a playboy who would never grow up. Then she'd said, "Lindy, you're a personal assistant to a man with too much money. He's never had to do a day of work in his life. That's not a job. In my book, that's called baby-sitting. Heck, because of this man you can't even have a real relationship with anyone. Craig's a nice guy and you've never really given him a chance. Just a few odd dates here and there."

No, for three years Lindy had given Shane the best of her, never once asking for anything in return. All other men paled when judged by the Shane factor.

Lindy looked at Shane, whose expression still showed that he was waiting for her answer. She searched desperately for the right words, finally settling on, "I think that I need more."

Shane moved across the room and stood close to her. "More what? Money? Done. You're the best assistant I've ever had. I'll pay you—" he named a figure that was astronomical, and more than what Grandpa Joe had offered earlier. In less than a minute he had practically doubled her salary.

"I—" Lindy choked as she tried to speak. The salary he'd offered would allow her to save for the down payment on a house. She'd be able to move herself into a comfortable financial position, one that would secure her future. Money was her absolutely weakest spot because she'd grown up with hardly any.

So, was she prostituting herself if she stayed? Could she stay with him for a short while longer? Resolve filled her as her mind overrode her emotions. She should take Shane's counteroffer back to Grandpa Joe. That's what she should do. She steeled herself. Yes, that's what any good businesswoman would do.

He must have sensed her indecision because he stepped forward and took her hands in his. Heat and warmth from his touch immediately spread through her. His gaze gently held hers. "Lindy, I need you. Stay."

Emotions poured through Lindy, overriding the common sense and mental control she'd been struggling to hang on to. Her ability to reason and think flew out the window. It had always been like that with Shane. All he ever had to do was touch her or look at her with those blue eyes, just as he was doing now, and she'd be swept away. She couldn't resist him.

He was her downfall.

"One month." The words escaped from her mouth, buying her time. "I'll decide at the end of a month. I'll give you at least one more month, and then decide after that what I'm going to do."

A jubilant smile lit up Shane's face, and Lindy turned her head away. He dropped her hands, allowing her a fraction more self-control as the heat from his touch subsided. "You know I'll convince you to stay longer."

"We'll see." She struggled to calm her racing heart.

Shane, however, was now back to business. "Since we have at least a month, can we now get things back to normal between us?"

She doubted things would ever be normal between them again. But what was one more lie? "Sure. Now I've got a lot of work to do. Those foundation requests that you were expecting arrived in today's mail. As soon as I process everything I'll get them ready for you."

"That sounds fine."

Lindy gathered her things and headed into the office. Up until today she'd always thought it was overly large. But now, with Shane's desk so close to hers, the space seemed impossibly small. How could she work right beside him?

One month. She could do one month. That would give her time to renegotiate the job with Grandpa Joe, and then make a move to Jacobsen Enterprises. She'd give herself one month to begin to heal her heart and say her final goodbyes to Shane.

"I REALLY DON'T THINK you should go to work today." Tina stood in the doorway to the apartment's hall bathroom. "Whatever you've got, Lindy, you've got it bad."

Lindy wiped her mouth on the wet washcloth that Tina handed her. "Really, I'll be fine. Those chicken taquitos we had for dinner yesterday just didn't sit well, I was burping them up all night."

Tina leaned over, averting her eyes as she flushed the toilet for Lindy. "Well, there they go, or at least their remnants."

Still clutching the washcloth to her lips, Lindy got to her feet. "I feel funny. Do I feel warm?"

Tina put her hand on Lindy's forehead. "No. No fever. I think you probably just had food poisoning."

"That's what I think, although I don't know why it didn't claim you, too."

"I only ate one of them. You had like six or seven. Anyway, why don't you go back to sleep? I'll call Shane and tell him you aren't coming. I'm going to be home all day, since my next flight assignment isn't until tomorrow morning."

Lindy's eyes widened in panic. "You can't call Shane! I can't call in sick. This Friday will end the month I promised him, and I'm giving him my two weeks notice. Until then, I don't want him to think that anything's wrong. You know I'm going to Jacobsen. He just doesn't know it yet."

Tina nodded. "And it's about time. But you really aren't well."

"It doesn't matter. I don't want him worried. I've got to go in. I've got so much to do. I want things to be settled by the time I tell Shane that I'm leaving. As it is he's not going to understand. We've had a pretty good truce this past month."

Lindy put the washcloth down and reached for her toothbrush and the toothpaste. "I'm sure I'll feel better now that all this stuff is out of my system."

"If you're sure. You call me if you need me. I can always come get you." Tina stepped out of the room. "That's what friends are for, you know."

Lindy studied her pale face in the mirror. Besides her stomach upheaval, her nose was stuffy. She pressed her fingers to the sides of her throat. About this time every year, she always ended up on antibiotics. She was allergic to something that arrived each spring and even though her glands weren't swollen yet, it must be getting close to that time. She'd give it another day and if she didn't feel better, she'd call her doctor.

SEVERAL HOURS and one package of Hostess Ho Ho's later, she was feeling much better. She took a drink of her bottled water and leaned back in satisfaction. She'd finally finished organizing all the files. They were in great shape for whomever took her place.

"Ho Ho's?" Shane remarked as he entered the office. "You've become quite the junk-food nut this past week. First M&M's and now Ho Ho's. What did you eat for lunch?''

"Caesar salad."

"Impressive. Where's your trademark banana?"

"I finished that earlier." Lindy looked up. As always, Shane was dressed in a polo shirt and jeans. "Is there something you need?"

"Yes. I need concert tickets and dinner reservations." He rattled off a name and a date at her and hastily Lindy wrote it on her scratch pad.

"How many?"

"Two. I'm taking Cathy Barnes."

Lindy looked up sharply. Having arrived in St. Louis a month ago, blond bombshell Cathy Barnes was the new gossip and sex-help columnist for one of St. Louis's alternative dailies. She also hosted a call-in radio talk show—*and was set on being Mrs. Shane Jacobsen.* Lindy had immediately hated her. "Is this a date?"

Shane looked up from the mail he was going through. "So what if it is?"

Lindy placed her hands carefully on the desk, gripping the edges of the cherry-wood surface for support. "Organizing your dates is no longer in my job description."

"And how is that different than if I was taking out a client?"

"You don't have any clients."

"Foundation people then," Shane argued. His jaw set stubbornly. "When did you get so difficult?"

She ignored that. "Take it or leave it. At least your

grandfather treats me like a professional and not a personal slave. I am not getting you concert tickets so that you can go out with Cathy Barnes. She's a snake.''

Shane's face creased in surprise. ''What is with you? If I didn't know you so well, I'd say you were jealous.''

Lindy flattened her palms against the smooth surface of the desk, in an attempt to regain some self-control. Jealous? Always. But she'd learned to live with it. Until she'd slept with Shane Jacobsen. Now the thought of him being with anyone else, especially after her, was unbearable. She trembled. Just two more weeks and she would be free of him, and hopefully able to put the green-eyed jealousy monster behind her.

''No.'' She stared at him, a sudden courage evident in her eyes. After all, what could he do? Fire her? She already had a new job.

Shane finally blinked, his expression telling her he didn't understand, or like, the situation at all. ''Fine. You don't have to get involved. I'll handle it myself.''

''Thank you.''

''Sure.'' Shane watched as Lindy turned back to her computer keyboard. Just what was up with her now? She was so unlike Lindy. The old Lindy never refused him anything, or ate junk food. Or looked so pale.

He didn't have time to think about it because just then an overseas call came through. But he did think about it an hour later when he decided not to call about the concert tickets. No, without Lindy running inter-ference, his dating life was about to go down the tubes.

He leaned back in his desk chair and studied her for a moment. He probably needed a break from the sin-gles scene anyway. Ever since Easter, Grandpa Joe had been sending e-mails about women he thought Shane should meet. Shane had refused to even ac-knowledge that he'd received the correspondence.

"I need to take this to the post office," Lindy said. She stood up. "Is there anything else you need?"

"No." And then he understood. He'd been right. Something was wrong. He knew it instinctively, and his instinct had never failed him. "Lindy? Are you okay?"

"I'm—" Lindy put a hand to her mouth, turned and made a run for it. Shane followed her to the bathroom and pressed his head against the closed door. The sounds coming from inside told him all he needed to know.

"I'm calling a doctor."

"I'm fine!"

Shane smiled despite himself. She was so stubborn. "You're hacking up a lung."

"And you're a hypochondriac. Really, I—" She stopped, overcome by another bout of nausea.

Shane grimaced. Lindy really was sick. He'd been right to trust his instincts. After all, it was his intuition that had made him millions on the stock market, and freed him from his beloved Grandpa Joe's tentacles.

To give Lindy some privacy, Shane went in search

of his cell phone and dialed his sister. "Hey, Bethany."

"Shane. What's up? You caught me right between patients."

"Lindy's sick. She's throwing up in my bathroom. Maybe I'm paranoid, but you know what happened to Dan. I'd better be safe than sorry."

"Yes, I remember. Hold that file a minute, Marge, it's my brother. Okay, I'm back. What are her symptoms?"

Shane paused. "She looks pale. She's not been eating right. She's throwing up."

"Does she have a fever?"

Did she? Shane frowned. "I don't think so. But her nose is very congested."

He heard Bethany sigh. "She's probably got a virus, Shane. It sounds like she just needs some rest. Tell her to take some decongestants for the stuffy nose and if she has a fever tell her to take two acetaminophen tablets every four hours. If she's not better in another twenty-four hours, or if she runs a fever, she needs to see her doctor."

Shane frowned. "That's it?"

His sister sounded busy. "Yes, unless she's pregnant."

"She's not pregnant."

"Then she's got a virus. Call me later if you need to, but right now I've got to go because I'm way off schedule."

"Thanks." Shane set the phone down and walked back to the bathroom door. "Lindy? Are you all right?'' He heard the telltale flushing and then the sound of water running in the sink.

"I'm fine," Lindy finally called. "I think it was the salad. The dressing must have had a lot of egg in it. You know I'm allergic to eggs in large amounts."

"Bethany says you probably have a virus. You need to rest and take acetaminophen."

Lindy opened the door. She looked even paler, if that were possible. Shane was really concerned now. He stepped aside to let her leave the bathroom.

"Maybe it's the yearly allergy thing I always get," she said. "Just a different variation this time."

"Or you could be pregnant."

HE MEANT IT as a joke to cheer her up, to lighten the moment. She could see the good intentions written all over his face. But his joke wasn't funny. Could she be pregnant? Fear filled her. Had Shane used a condom? She couldn't remember. No. She couldn't be pregnant. Fate couldn't be so cruel. Sure, she wanted children, but not now. Not like this.

"I'm not pregnant," Lindy said, but doubt crept into her mind and took root. After all, she was late. But her cycle being late was nothing new. Not every woman's cycle ran like clockwork, and Lindy was often as much as fifteen days late. She gave Shane a reassuring smile, although her mind was hardly reassured. "Stop being worried. I'm fine now. I'm sure it was just the egg in the Caesar salad."

He didn't look convinced. "I want you to take the rest of the day off. Go home. Rest. Sleep."

"Really, I have those letters to do and—"

"They'll wait. I insist you go home." Shane followed her to her desk. Lindy took a long sip of water. Her stomach again felt queasy.

"You know I'm going to win this battle," he said quietly.

A small smile crept onto Lindy's face. She did know. When his friend Dan had started having strange symptoms it had been Shane who had insisted Dan go to the hospital. Shane's paranoia had saved Dan's life. At moments like this, it was one of his best attributes. Even though she knew she didn't have meningitis as Dan had, Lindy caved. "You win. I'm going home. I'll see you in the morning."

"Do you want me to drive you?"

Lindy's heart overflowed. Sometimes Shane could be so thoughtful. If only—she pushed those fantasies out of her head. In two weeks, she'd be out of Shane's life forever. She had to remember that she was just his employee. "That's sweet, but really I'll be fine."

His brow furrowed. "Okay, but if you need anything you call me."

"Sure," Lindy replied. For one last moment she let herself revel in Shane's concern.

He smiled at her. "Go home."

"Going," Lindy said. Fifteen minutes later she pulled into the drugstore parking lot. She glanced at herself in the rearview mirror. Before she'd only looked pale. Now she looked afraid.

Could she be pregnant? Shane's words had planted the idea in her head, and once she'd gotten to her car she'd thought of nothing else. And she *was* queasy, throwing up, and late with her monthly cycle.

She reached up and felt her throat. Her glands were normal. She blinked. This was all going to turn out fine. Just fine.

She went into the store. Minutes later, she exited with a pregnancy test that promised results in as little as three minutes. She'd also bought a jumbo-size bag of Hershey Kisses, her favorite stress food. After all, it was Murphy's Law. Be prepared for the worst and it wouldn't happen to you. Or something like that.

It seemed like forever, instead of the five minutes it actually took her to reach the parking space at her apartment. She walked up the two flights of stairs to her third-floor apartment. The May day was perfect—sunny, no humidity, in the low seventies. But Lindy couldn't appreciate anything, not with this cloud of impending doom hanging over her head.

She dropped the bag of foil-wrapped chocolates on the kitchen counter and headed into the bathroom. After reading the directions, she took the test.

Her cell phone shrilled and Lindy left the bathroom to get it. Her shoulders slumped as she read the caller ID. Shane. She certainly didn't need him showing up on her doorstep again. Not today. She answered the call. "Hello."

"Hi. I wanted to make sure you got home okay."

"I did," Lindy said. She walked back into the bathroom. The pregnancy test was exactly where she'd left it, lying on the countertop, white plastic on beige Formica.

Shane's warm baritone rumbled in her ear. "So how are you feeling? Any better? You've crawled into bed, haven't you?"

"Uh, yes," Lindy stammered, her attention diverted by the lines forming in each of the test windows. The pink line in the larger window confirmed the test was complete. The pink line in the other window meant—

Lindy let her legs collapse out from under her as she slid down the bathroom door. Her rear hit the cool tile and she leaned back against the doorframe.

"Lindy? Are you feeling better? Do you need anything? I can be there in twenty minutes. I'm worried about you. You are feeling better, right?"

No. Lindy closed her eyes. She wouldn't be feeling like herself again for nine months. And she never would be free of Shane Jacobsen. Not when she was having his baby.

"I'm fine, Shane," she lied. "I'm just fine."

Chapter Three

"Oh, my God! No wonder you were so sick yesterday! You're pregnant!"

Uh-oh. Lindy winced before glancing over to watch Tina storm out of the bathroom, positive pregnancy test in hand. "Put down that pancake syrup and tell me the truth, Melinda Jean Brinks! This is yours, isn't it, which means that you are pregnant!"

"Yes," Lindy said. All night she'd been patting her flat stomach, imagining the changes she couldn't yet feel—changes she knew would be evident in just a few months. Lindy spoke again, as if by telling her best friend she made it even more real. "Yes, I'm pregnant."

To avoid Tina's speculative gaze, Lindy let the syrup run over the pancakes. The trash bag rustled, indicating that Tina had disposed of the test.

Pancakes ready, Lindy used breakfast as an excuse to step out of Tina's orbit. Once married herself, Tina was a take-charge, no-nonsense woman whom Lindy often envied. Tina wouldn't waffle; she'd just keep going straight ahead the way she had when her husband had started cheating on her. Lindy sat at the tiny kitchen table, the small bite of pancake tasting papery against her tongue.

"I don't know if I want to know," Tina said, breaking the short silence, "but you know I must. On a hopeful note, Craig's?"

"You know I don't feel anything for him," Lindy said, her focus still on her plate. "I feel guilty enough that he likes me, but I can't get into him. I haven't seen him for two months and never once did I do more than kiss him good-night."

"So that means it's…"

"Shane's," Lindy confirmed. She glanced up in time to see the look of disapproval that crossed Tina's face when she heard Shane's name. Lindy quickly continued, "But he doesn't know."

"He doesn't know." Tina's tone changed abruptly as the implications of that revelation set in. "If he doesn't know, then what are you planning on doing? Surely, no—"

"No. I'm having this baby," Lindy said hurriedly. "I will not have an abortion, nor will I have the baby and give it away."

The former had been something Tina had done when she was twenty, and regretted to this very day. When Lindy had lain awake all night, contemplating, she'd known that, without a doubt, she'd never terminate a pregnancy. She'd manage—somehow.

Tina's voice cut through the sudden silence. "I'm glad. But, since you're planning on having this baby, you are planning on telling Shane, aren't you?"

The words were out before Lindy could think to stop them. "He doesn't even know that we had sex."

Tina thumped onto the chair opposite Lindy. She pushed back a wayward strand of her brunette hair. "I really think you need to tell me about this."

Lindy stabbed at a piece of pancake, although she didn't lift it to her lips. "There's really nothing to tell. He threw that party for his birthday, and fool that I am, after he called me, I went. He'd been mixing alcohol and painkillers, and I got way too drunk. End of story. I, like most stupid women, succumbed to the Shane Jacobsen playboy charm."

"And..."

Lindy dropped the fork and pushed her barely touched breakfast plate away. "Best sex of my life and he doesn't remember a thing."

"Oh, honey!" Tina reached over and enveloped Lindy in a huge bear hug. "I'm so sorry. But haven't I been warning you about him?"

"Yes, and I admit it, I knew better." Tears brimmed in Lindy's eyes but she sniffed them back. No more tears. She'd cried enough over Shane Jacobsen. "You're right, I know better! But I couldn't help it. It was like someone took over my body and set me free to indulge in my greatest fantasy. And indulge I did. And I know I have no excuse for my behavior."

"That's good, I guess," Tina acknowledged.

"But I love him. Or is it just obsession? Whatever it is, he's my Willoughby. You know, like in *Sense and Sensibility*? I know he's wrong for me, but I can't help myself from caring. Why can't I be sensible?"

"Lindy, it's okay to admit you love him, and it's okay to hurt." Tina pulled Lindy closer. "I know you love him, and believe me, he doesn't deserve you. I wish that somehow you'd find that Colonel Brandon who will love you. I know he's out there, and you know I'll be here for you, like always, whatever you decide."

"I know. Thank you." Lindy let herself rest in her best friend's arms, the way she'd been doing ever since high school.

"Nothing has an easy answer anymore," Lindy finally said. "My pregnancy will be obvious in a short while. It's not like I can hide it!"

"Shh," Tina said gently. She drew back slightly. "You've got a little time to figure things out. And this apartment is big enough for a baby. At least for now. And you have that new job to consider. The pay will be a big help. So eat your breakfast."

"I just hope it stays down," Lindy said as Tina pushed the plate of pancakes back in front of her.

"It will," Tina said. "Think positive. For a while, Shane won't know. And if nothing else, you can always tell him the baby's someone else's."

Lindy shot Tina a dirty look. "Okay, scratch that," Tina said. "Just when is your last day again?"

"Like I told you, I'm giving my notice tomorrow. That way I will have stayed a month, like I told him I would."

"Well, that's something to be thankful about," Tina said, more to comfort herself than Lindy. "So let's think positive. After about two weeks you'll never have to see Shane again. After all, he never goes to Jacobsen Enterprises and I doubt he ever will, not so long as he can spite his grandfather with it. Now, my dear, I have to go to work. I'm actually on local flights for a while, running back and forth from here to Chicago. Leave a message on my cell phone if you need me. I get a thirty-minute break between flights.''

"Okay.''

Tina stood. "Lindy?''

Lindy looked up and Tina smiled. "Stop feeling sorry for yourself, honey. You are a survivor, and you're going to have a baby.'' Tina's face clouded for a moment and then her expression softened. "And as much as I hate to say it, it's Shane's baby and you love him. You have to tell him.''

Panic gripped Lindy. Yes, it was the right thing to do, telling Shane. But not now. Not until she had herself together. Not until she freed herself from her lovesick obsession with Shane. And rid herself of the Shane-standard she judged other men by. Maybe then she could tell him. But not now. She took a steadying breath.

"I can't tell him, Tina. I don't want my baby to suffer visitation like I had to. I don't want my baby passed between two parents and get caught up in their endless differences. No, I don't want that, not even for the child support money. I thought of that last night. No joint custody. It's best he not know. I'm not going to tell him.''

"I still think you should tell him. Who knows? Maybe he'll do the right thing and marry you,'' Tina said, without much enthusiasm. "Even I have to admit that although he's a playboy, he is a Jacobsen and they do have a tendency to do the right thing."

And how often had Lindy thought of that? Being Mrs. Shane Jacobsen was her wildest dream. But trapping Shane into it? Never.

"I tortured myself with that too," Lindy said. "I could be Mrs. Shane Jacobsen. But he doesn't love me. He doesn't love anyone. I mean, look at all those other women. Make love with Shane Jacobsen and it's a ticket to flowers, jewelry and a quick goodbye. And I don't want a loveless marriage, or to expose my child or myself to a philanderer. I'd rather be alone."

"He could grow to love you. You've sung his praises, and you do know him better than I do. You're the one who's worked successfully with him for three years."

"Please. A little reality check here. I'm his PA, his girl Friday who does the mundane chores that he could do himself if he wanted to. He only needs me because it makes him look as if he's really working, contributing. He's just too rich to think of lowering himself to do the work I do."

"Lindy! I never heard you talk this way. You've never painted Shane so bad."

Lindy took a cleansing breath and tried to rein in her emotions, without success. "No, I'm not overreacting. He's a clueless, spoiled man. I doubt he could ever have feelings for me, I'm so far from what he thinks his ideal woman is. No, I couldn't stand myself taking him away from his dream woman. Even if I don't think she really exists, it's not right to trap him into marriage. We'd end up driving each other crazy, hating each other. Best he never know.''

Tina's expression was sympathetic. "Lindy, think about it a little more. Don't make any rash decisions. I'll talk to you tonight. I'll be home. Let's do spaghetti. I'll cook.''

Lindy smiled for the first time since she'd discovered she was pregnant. Spaghetti and microwave popcorn were the only things Tina could cook. "Okay, you're on. I'm sure there's a jar of sauce here somewhere.''

"Great. I'll pick up some French bread and a bag of tossed salad on the way home. I want you to hang in there and call me if you need me.'' With that, Tina disappeared from the kitchen.

Lindy looked at the microwave clock and grimaced. She got up and scraped the uneaten pancakes into the trash can. Breakfast was over. It was time to go face Shane Jacobsen.

"HEY, HOW ARE you feeling?''

"Great,'' Lindy lied as she stepped into the living room of the pool house about thirty minutes later. "Must have been a twenty-four-hour bug or something.''

Shane's blue eyes narrowed as he ran his gaze over her. Lindy tried not to flush, and she was relieved that he seemed to buy her story. "You do look a lot better. There's a bit of a glow on your cheeks. That's a good sign, isn't it?''

"Yes," Lindy replied. She brushed past him, deliberately averting her eyes so that she couldn't see up close how his suit flattered his body. She could still remember touching him, as if the dastardly, decadent deed had just been done yesterday and not over a month ago.

Just two more weeks. She could survive two more weeks of seeing Shane everyday. Right?

"What did you say?" She turned toward Shane. He was grabbing his briefcase.

"I said we need to hurry or we'll be late. Remember? We have to be off-site today for meetings. Grab your stuff."

Lindy nodded. In all the anxiety about her situation, she'd forgotten she had a hectic workday ahead of her.

Shane had already taken one step out of the door. "We'll do lunch somewhere downtown. If you have any preferences let me know. It'll make up for having to stop by Jacobsen Enterprises today. Unfortunately, Grandfather beckons."

He did? Lindy frowned. That was new. But she didn't have time to question Shane further. Instead, she grabbed everything she needed, and then, for the rest of the morning and early afternoon, the day passed as if nothing had ever changed between them.

Despite what she'd told Tina, Shane did "work." Together, they spent the morning touring inner-city child-care centers and attending board meetings. At each stop, Shane impressed Lindy by the way he truly listened to the various organizations' requests for Shane Jacobsen Foundation funding.

Even lunch at Kemoll's went well. The fettuccini Alfredo was al dente, and she successfully managed to keep it all down. At three o'clock sharp, she and Shane arrived at Jacobsen Enterprises.

With its tropical-oasis look, complete with waterfall, the immense multi-story atrium lobby in Grandpa Joe's headquarters never failed to impress Lindy. She automatically glanced back over her shoulder to where the portraits of Joe Jacobsen, CEO, and his son-in-law, Andrew Sanders, President, hung over the entry doors. On another wall were logos from the various companies that made up Jacobsen Enterprises: Grandpa Joe's Good Eats; Jocobsen's, a chain of restaurants; the signature eatery, Henrietta's; a restaurant-supply firm and a microbrewery. A small chill passed through her. This was where she was going to work.

"Mr. Jacobsen." The cute little receptionist seemed slightly flustered as Shane approached, and as always Lindy felt her annoyance grow. Yes, Shane did look handsome in his custom-tailored suit and, yes, his surfer-blond hair and charm and natural good looks were appealing. But did every woman he ran into have to act like a star-struck teenager?

"Oh yes, Mr. Jacobsen, I saw you coming so I've had the executive elevator sent down for you." The receptionist smiled a bit too brightly for Lindy's taste, and she wished the myopic Plain Jane that used to sit behind the desk hadn't been promoted.

"Thank you," Shane replied with a warm smile of his own, while the receptionist blushed. Lindy set her own lips in a politely professional line as she followed

Shane. Every time Shane visited Jacobsen, Grandpa Joe insisted he use the executive elevator. Since Shane didn't work for the company, the lift had to be sent down to pick him up.

Of course, when she went to work for Jacobsen, she would be in the regular elevators like everyone else. Her little cubicle would be nowhere near the executive floor.

They stepped inside the lift, and the ride to the executive floor was quick.

"Hello, Shane," Grandpa Joe's secretary said as she rose to greet them. "He's waiting for you. Mr. Sanders is already with him."

"Thank you."

Within moments, Lindy had a courtside view as Shane discussed his grandfather's latest idea, blending some of his personal foundation bequests with those of Jacobsen Enterprises. Watching the men interact fascinated Lindy. Didn't Shane know how good he was at holding his own with the two men? Did he not see the potential that he had to do even more by working with his family instead of against them?

An hour later, the meeting ended when Andrew, Grandpa Joe and Shane had wrapped up the last bit of business. Shane turned toward her, and Lindy shuffled some papers to avoid eye contact. "Lindy? I've got to go to Andrew's office for a moment. You can come with me or—"

"She can wait here," Grandpa Joe interrupted. "Didn't you tell me that she's been sick? Don't make her do more than necessary, Shane."

"I'll wait here," Lindy said.

"We'll only be a moment," Andrew reassured her, as he closed the doors.

"Ah," Grandpa Joe said as he returned to sit next to her on the leather couch. "Now that we're alone we can finally talk openly. Have you told Shane of your situation yet?"

"No," Lindy admitted. "I plan on giving him my two weeks notice tomorrow. I'll tell him then that I'm coming to work for you."

Grandpa Joe's Jacobsen blue eyes darkened slightly. "Oh no, dear. You misunderstood me. I'm not worried about your leaving Shane. I wanted to know if you'd told him that you're having a baby."

Lindy's jaw dropped open. "Baby? What baby?"

Grandpa Joe reached over and patted her hand. "Oh, my dear. I'm sorry again. I poleaxed you, I guess. But you see, I have a gift about these things. I always know when there's a Jacobsen baby on the way. I knew with Henrietta's, Lilly's, and I even knew before Sara did that she was pregnant with Shane. I'd say you're due in January and that you're having a boy. So I take it you haven't told Shane that he's going to be a father?"

"Shane is, I didn't, I…" Lindy faltered.

Grandpa Joe patted her hand again. "You've worked for him for three years and even though he's too dumb to see what's right in front of his nose, I'm not. I'm guessing it was you that left that little mark on his neck, and that at the same time he left you a small present." Grandpa Joe reached for the leather container that held tissue. "Now don't cry, Lindy. This isn't a tragedy. I'd be honored to have you for an in-law."

To stop the tears, Lindy blew her nose. "He doesn't even know."

"Well, of course not. But you'll tell him about the baby, he'll do the right thing and marry you, and you'll both live happily ever after. That's how these things work. Trust me."

"He doesn't even know we had sex." Lindy pulled her hand out of Grandpa Joe's and covered her face. "I shouldn't have. I didn't mean…"

"Why don't you tell me about it." The tone of Grandpa Joe's voice brooked no arguments, and Lindy knew she didn't have a choice. After making Grandpa Joe promise not to tell Shane about the baby, she quickly filled him in on the whole situation.

"So, you see, I can't tell him and I don't want him trapped into marrying me. He doesn't love me, and I won't settle for less."

"I can respect that," Grandpa Joe said. He nodded thoughtfully and refilled Lindy's glass of water. "But eventually you'll have to tell Shane. He will figure it out, you know."

"Perhaps. But I can't tell him now. Not now. It'll take all my strength just to quit working for him."

"I understand," Grandpa Joe said. "And luckily for all involved, you're coming to work here. We have an excellent on-site child-care center, excellent health benefits, and your job will allow you to work flexible hours. We were named one of *Working Mother*'s top companies to work for, you know.''

''I know,'' Lindy said.

''So that's all taken care of. You'll be fine, and I'm here if you need me. I know you told Shane that employees weren't family, but since you're carrying my great-grandchild, I think it's close enough.''

''Thank you,'' Lindy said.

''Anytime,'' Grandpa Joe said. ''Now, if I'm correct, here come Shane and Andrew.''

Within moments the two men walked back through the double mahogany doors. Shane looked worried when he saw the two of them seated close together.

''You haven't been trying to steal her away again, have you?'' Shane asked.

''Now why would I do that?'' Grandpa Joe replied. He rose and gave Lindy a knowing look. ''You both take care.''

''We will,'' Lindy replied as she followed Shane from the office.

''So did he?'' Shane asked as they took the elevator back to the lobby.

''Did he what?''

''Try to steal you away?''

''He doesn't have to,'' Lindy admitted. Shane had given her the opening she needed and she paused as they stepped out into the atrium. ''I told him a month ago that I was accepting his job offer.''

''You're joking,'' Shane said. He turned to fully face her, his confusion evident. ''I gave you a raise, which you took.''

Lindy twisted her hands together. "And I gave you a month, as promised. But tomorrow I am putting in my two weeks notice."

"You can't do this. Lindy, I need you!"

People were turning to look at them, so Shane ushered Lindy toward the doors. "We'll talk about this in the car," he said.

But during the car ride home, an awkward silence fell over them. When they reached the driveway of the pool house, he parked the car, killed the engine and turned to her. "So you're going."

"Yes," Lindy said. She avoided his gaze by looking out the front windshield. "Shane, I have to go. It's been a great three years but I need more. I need to use all of my talents and skills. I need to use my degree. It's time that each of us moves on."

Shane drummed his fingers on the leather-wrapped steering wheel of his Corvette. "How much will it take for you to stay?"

"You can't buy me this time," Lindy replied. She turned to him, her eyes pleading with him to understand. The inside of the car suddenly felt stifling as his face remained impassive.

"Please understand that I have to go, Shane. Two weeks from now—that is, if you want me to stay the two weeks—I'm going to work for Jacobsen. Even though I don't have an MBA, I do have a business degree. I've even been accepted into the Jacobsen Stars program."

"Congratulations," Shane said flatly, the look on his face indicating he really didn't mean it. "And if I know you, you've got everything ready so that if you walk out of here tomorrow, any temp could walk right in and pick right up.''

"Yes," Lindy replied. "I can call the agency and have them arrange for some candidate interviews. I know you found me at your broker's office, but there are several very reputable employment agencies that will help you find my permanent replacement."

"I'll take care of it," Shane said. He turned his body so that he faced her. "I tell you what, how about we just split the difference. Work next week and I'll give you the following week off with pay. Sort of a vacation for having to put up with me these past three years."

Lindy sighed. She hated that he felt wounded. "It hasn't been a chore."

Shane gave her a curt nod and opened the car door. "It's late. Why don't you go home? In fact, let's take tomorrow off. After all, Monday's Memorial Day, so let's just make it a four-day weekend. I'll just see you Tuesday."

He came around and opened Lindy's car door. Fire flared between their fingertips as he assisted her out of the car.

"Tuesday," Shane repeated. And then he was gone, disappearing into the pool house. Lindy jumped slightly as the parked Corvette beeped and its lights flashed. Shane had obviously set the car alarm from inside the pool house.

Lindy stared at the car, and then at the pool-house door. St. Louis was on daylight savings time, meaning that the days had grown longer. For that reason, she couldn't tell if Shane had turned on any lights.

She rummaged for her car keys, inserted them into her Grand Prix, and drove the rest of the way home in tears.

"I DIDN'T EXPECT you to still be here."

Grandpa Joe looked up as Andrew Sanders stepped into Grandpa Joe's executive office. "I had some things to finish."

"Yes, but it's almost six-thirty. I thought Henrietta banned you from working any more late nights."

"She's playing bridge tonight so she won't know," Grandpa Joe said. "Besides, I've been thinking."

Andrew grinned. "Uh-oh. That's dangerous. Profitable, but usually very dangerous. So what's got you so worked up this time?"

"Lindy's pregnant with Shane's baby."

Andrew sat in the wing-back leather chair located across from Grandpa Joe's huge mahogany desk. "I won't even say 'you're kidding' because I can see that you're not. I didn't know they were seeing each other."

Grandpa Joe stroked his beard, a habit when he was problem-solving. "That's the whole problem. They aren't. He mixed pain pills and alcohol at his birthday party, and when he kissed her... Well, you know all about the birds and bees. It's obvious to everyone but him that she loves him. So at the party she had a few drinks herself and things happened."

"At his birthday party?"

"I just said that."

"I just wanted to be clear. After all, they've worked together for three years."

"Nothing ever happened until that night," Grandpa Joe confirmed.

Andrew shook his head as he comprehended it all. "So what do you plan on doing about it?"

"I don't know." Grandpa Joe whirled in his big leather chair and looked east down Market Street toward the Mississippi riverfront. The position of the sun caused the steel of the western face of the Gateway Arch to shimmer. Usually the sight inspired him, but this time inspiration deserted him. For once he wasn't exactly sure what to do.

Andrew's voice cut through Grandpa Joe's contemplations. "You don't have any objections to Lindy, do you?"

Grandpa Joe whirled back to face his son-in-law. It never ceased to amaze Grandpa Joe that he was closer to his daughter's husband than to Blake, his own son. "I have no objections at all. I adore Lindy. She's perfect for him. She fits him. I have no objection to welcoming her as a permanent member of this family. But she doesn't want him if he doesn't love her. And you know Shane. He wouldn't know love if it bit him right in the rear end."

Andrew nodded. "True."

"Even worse, that boy's as stubborn as a Missouri mule, which means that I'm going to have to be very underhanded here. She told me I couldn't tell him, so I'm going to split hairs here. He has to know, but technically I'm not going to be the one to tell him. Well, not directly.''

Andrew waved his hands in a stop motion. ''Don't look at me. I'm not going to tell him.''

''No, you're safe. This situation is so delicate that it must not be able to be traced back to me or to you. It has to be handled with the ultimate finesse.'' Grandpa Joe paused as his idea took shape. ''I've got it. We need Marvin Judson. He's the only one we can trust.''

Andrew made a face. ''Ew. You really want to bring Marvin in on this? Marvin's slime.''

Grandpa Joe nodded and his Santa-Claus-like beard bobbed. ''Yes. I want Marvin. He owes me a small favor, and despite his sleazeball reputation, I happen to know he can be discreet.'' Grandpa Joe saw Andrew's look. ''Well, at least about his sources. He's going to have to be, for all our sakes.''

Andrew made himself comfortable by settling deeper into the chair. ''You know that Blake and Sara aren't going to like this.''

Grandpa Joe leaned forward and grabbed a pen. He made a notation on a memo pad. ''I know they won't like it. I don't like it, either. I don't want to handle it this way. It's not going to be pleasant. That's why no one but us can know. Yes, we need Marvin. He's the best man for the job. And I promise you, the ends will justify the means. It has to be done. If there was any other way…'' Grandpa Joe paused. ''There isn't, is there?''

''When?''

"Tuesday. We'll give them the holiday weekend. That's only fair, don't you think? Some calm before the storm?"

Andrew shook his head slightly. "You never cease to amaze me. I bet this one's going to cost."

Grandpa Joe smiled slightly and spun to look at the Arch again. His voice held sadness. "It always does, Andrew. It always does."

Chapter Four

HOT GOSSIP: Wayward Playboy knocks up PA
By Marvin Judson
People in the News Editor; St. Louis edition, *National Tattler*

Shane Jacobsen, wayward and prodigal son of world-famous evangelical minister Blake Jacobsen and his wife, Sara, has committed the ultimate sin. It seems the youngest son of the dynamic ministry duo has succeeded in getting his PA, Melinda Brinks, pregnant, reliable sources confirmed yesterday. Shane Jacobsen is also the grandson of Joe Jacobsen, CEO of Jacobsen Enterprises. Brinks is due in January.

Spokesmen for Blake Jacobsen Ministries have refused to comment on the situation, and neither Shane Jacobsen nor Brinks could be reached for comment.

In other St. Louis personality news, local broadcaster Larry—

THE INSISTENT RINGING woke Shane from the deep sleep he'd been in. He rolled over and slammed his fist on the snooze button, only to discover that it wasn't the clock that had dragged him out of his fabulous dream.

Wait! Shane attempted to kiss Julia Roberts one last time but she was slipping away, fading into the sharp morning sunlight now filtering through the white miniblinds. The clock blinked 7:07. He lunged for the telephone that was still creating an infernal racket on the bedside table.

"Hello?"

"Shane Jacobsen! How could you? I don't believe what you've done!"

Uh-oh. He knew that voice and *that* tone. "Hello, Mom."

His mind suddenly perfectly clear, Shane sat up in bed, the sheet slipping down to reveal his bare chest. He cocked the receiver against his ear and reached for a pair of boxers. It was always best to be somewhat dressed when dealing with his mother, even if she was literally half a world away in Australia. He grunted a few times as he pulled the shorts on, using only one hand.

"Shane? What's that noise? Are you even awake yet?" His mother's voice was shrill. "Don't you ever get up?"

"It's only seven here," Shane countered, but from her "Uh" sound he knew his mother would have none of it. He noticed a sinking feeling in his gut. Whatever he'd done, it was huge. She never exhaled like that.

"So, young man, what do you have to say for yourself this time?"

How many times in his twenty-five years had he heard those words? Shane blinked, and with his free hand he tried to straighten out his bed-head hairstyle. Hopeless. He sighed and scratched a spot of early-morning beard growth. No use in putting off the inevitable lecture. "Why don't you tell me what it is, Mother."

"What it is! You can't seriously be joking in a situation like this! What it is! Shane, you're in every gossip rag over here and quite a few over there, from what I understand. Didn't we teach you anything? While we certainly don't condone your lifestyle and actually abhor it, it is after all your choice when it comes to the way you want to live your life. But you could at least be discreet! You have a responsibility to your family and right now your father is the laughing-stock of the evangelical community. What did you do? Don't even attempt to wiggle your way out of this one. Do you really hate us this much?"

Shane slumped slightly, his brow furrowing as he racked his brain for some answer, some recent sin he'd committed to smear the family name again. His mind remained blank, just like after his birthday party. Surely this didn't have anything to do with his birthday party. That had been almost six weeks ago.

He heard his mother speaking to someone in the background. "What, Elise? You're kidding. Yes, we'll have to make a statement. Yes, we need damage control."

Sara came back onto the line, guns blazing. "I don't have time for this game, Shane. In no uncertain terms, you will marry the girl."

Marry? What? Shane sat up straighter. His mother had his full attention now. "What do you mean marry the girl?"

His mother's voice was deliberately cool. "Shane, this may be the twenty-first century, but in our family we honor our obligations. If you get someone pregnant, you marry them."

"Wait a minute here. I did not get anyone pregnant. I haven't had sex in—"

His mother cut him off. "Oh shut up, Shane. For once grow up. You did too have sex. With your PA of all people. And she's pregnant. Your grandfather even confirmed it when Blake called him a few minutes ago."

Oh, my God. Shane sat back against the headboard with a thump. Lindy sick. Bethany's words—"unless she's pregnant." Lindy's refusal to be friends.

But they'd made love when? Shane fisted the sheet and, suddenly, his memory—which to that moment had been so black—shone through with a bright white light. Only this light was attached to a train, and the locomotive slammed into him as the memory of his birthday fully returned.

He could see her now, underneath him, her face beautiful as he drove himself into her again and again. The phone fell from his hand as he remembered her passionate kisses, her mouth sweet like the finest honey. His fingers touched the place on his neck where the mark had been, and he could again hear her kittenish cries as he filled her and brought her to rapture's edge. The night had been magical, and the full impact of it hit him as the memory of their lovemaking returned.

He felt his face flush red. He'd made love to Lindy all right. More than once. His body strained uncomfortably as he remembered the bliss of it all. He shifted, forcing his arousal to cease. No wonder she'd been so distant and cold the day after his birthday.

He'd made endless love to her, and the next morning forgotten all about it.

"Shane! Shane!" His mother's insistent cries brought Shane back, away from that night, and he scrambled for the phone. "Shane!"

He put the receiver back to his ear. "Yes."

"I've been asking you what you plan to do."

He gave her the only answer he had. "I don't know."

"You two haven't talked?" Sara's voice conveyed her disbelief.

Up until this moment, I didn't realize we'd been together. Shane stretched his leg, popping his knee. While that pain felt better, he had other, serious problems that couldn't be fixed so easily. No, if Lindy was pregnant, and it was all over the press that world-famous evangelical minister Blake Jacobsen was about to have a grandchild out of wedlock, then it was probably not a good idea to tell his mother he didn't even remember the blessed event.

"Look, Mom, Lindy has not yet informed me of her

condition.'' Of course, now that the press had the story, he had no doubt she would be spilling the beans the moment she walked in the door. He'd make sure of it. Shane hated surprises, and this was the worst kind.

Sara didn't like that answer. ''What do you mean she hasn't told you yet?''

''She hasn't told me,'' Shane repeated stubbornly.

''Well, you're going to talk to her today. And marry her. What?'' His mother's voice faded off, and Shane knew she was listening to her assistant. ''You're kidding. Shane, CNN has just picked up this story. Only thirty seconds' worth on the air, according to Elise, but still enough to damage everything your father has worked for. I hate to use the word *famous,* Shane, but that's what he is. He's a minister leading people to Christ and Christian values, and your actions are the furthest thing from!''

''Judge not the prodigal son,'' Shane quipped.

''This isn't funny, Shane. People in other countries take these things very seriously. You must do the right thing. The whole world will be watching. Say you've had a secret engagement for the past year. She's your PA. Everyone will believe it.''

Shane frowned. He wasn't marrying anyone any more than he was planning on working for Jacobsen. Perhaps this was all some big cosmic joke of Grandpa Joe's. Shane reached for the remote, flipped on CNN, and discovered he must have timed it correctly, for there at the bottom of *Headline News,* running in the ticker tape, was the notice that he'd knocked up his

PA. Even Grandpa Joe wouldn't publicly embarrass his son just to play a joke on Shane.

But marry Lindy, even if she *was* pregnant? Shane turned off the television and fisted the covers. He didn't need his mother to give him the reasons for marriage. He and Lindy got along. They'd obviously had phenomenal sex. They'd been best friends for three years. They'd made a baby. But marry her? He didn't have those kinds of long-term lovey-dovey romantic feelings for her and he doubted that she did for him, either. Did a baby make a marriage? And would she even say yes?

"Shane, you have a responsibility here," his mother suddenly snapped, her impatience with his silence obvious. "You listen to me, son. You made a child. You are no longer important. The baby is. You must marry Lindy and provide my grandchild with a stable home!"

"I don't even know if Lindy would marry me," Shane said.

"Of course she would. She's female and she's pregnant. She obviously cares about you or she wouldn't have put up with you and your horrid shenanigans for the past three years."

"The only reason we got into bed in the first place is we were both too drunk to know any better," Shane said flatly.

He heard his mother's fast intake of breath. "Shane Jacobsen! This is your worst atrocity yet. If I were there I'd…"

Shane grimaced. Okay, telling his mother he'd been

drunk hadn't been a good idea. But it had just sort of slipped out. And could his morning be any worse? In less than fifteen minutes he'd just learned who'd left the hickey on his neck, and that she'd been lying to him about everything for over a month. And topping it off was the fact that she was pregnant.

"Mom," Shane said slowly, "you've always acknowledged to the world that I'm your wayward prodigal son. So what happened to the truth? Work that angle again. You know, we forgive him and all that jazz. Dad's always milked it for what it's worth. You know, prodigal son messes up again. You know, a lesson in forgiveness."

"The prodigal son realized his mistakes and corrected them," Sara shot back. "And we do not milk you for the good of our ministry! But God calls us to lead by example, and your father and I would just prefer it if you would exhibit some godly behaviors now and then. Is that too much for parents to ask? It's like everything that you do is only to spite us."

Silence descended, and Shane heard his mother's agitated breathing. Finally she spoke. "Shane, this isn't about your father and I having a world-renowned ministry. Yes, your indiscretions reflect badly on us, but we can take that type of a setback. Yes, your father can use this to show how to forgive. Because he does, after all, forgive you. You are our son and we both love you very much. Families are not perfect, not even ours. It will not tarnish his reputation permanently and, yes, after a while the gossip will die down. He will still lead by example. But Shane, the end result is the same. You've fathered a child. You are responsible for creating a life. You need to do the right thing by Lindy. We love you, Shane, but we will expect nothing less.'' Silence and then, ''Okay, Elise. I'm coming. Did you hear what I said, Shane?''

''Yes.''

''Good. I will call you later tonight to see what is happening. Goodbye, darling.''

And with that, the phone in his hand went dead. Shane set the receiver back on the base unit and flipped on the television again. He had only to wait about three minutes before the news anchor informed the world about his current indiscretions.

Shane sighed. If he'd had any other father in the world. But he had been fated to be none other than Blake Jacobsen's son, the Blake Jacobsen who prayed with world leaders and who held audiences with the Pope.

And once again Shane had failed. Well, he could look at it positively. He'd succeeded in being the screwup up that he'd always been. He'd done something that his parents had probably always dreaded—maybe even expected—would happen one day or another.

Sarcasm doesn't become you, Shane, he told himself as he headed for the shower. And this was one time that he didn't want to be a victor.

''SO YOU'RE DOWN to only one week?''

''Just one,'' Lindy replied. She pressed the washcloth to her mouth, wiping away the remnants of leftover toothpaste. ''Although, unlike work, the doctor says I can have at least five more weeks of this wonderful morning sickness.''

Tina peered at Lindy's face. ''Well, you shouldn't be sick any more today. You'll be fine.''

Lindy gave her friend a wan smile. ''Except that now I'm running late.''

Tina shrugged. ''So? What's he going to do, fire you?''

''Ha-ha, Tina. I know there is no love lost between you two, but Shane has nothing to do with my paranoia about being late. You know I hate being late for anything and I have to stop and put gas in the car. I'm driving on fumes.''

Tina blinked but refused to concede. ''Well, get a banana or something when you stop. You've got to keep up on your nutrition.''

''Yes, Mother,'' Lindy said with a wry smile. Between Tina and Shane, she was well looked after. The smile faded from Lindy's face, and she shook her head to clear the disturbing thought that in one week Shane wouldn't be around any longer. She gave herself a quick mental pep talk. She had to remember that leaving Shane was for the best.

Ten minutes later, Lindy knew why she never bought gas in the morning. The lineup was terrible. As she waited to pay for her purchases, she glanced at the newsstand. Nothing of great interest there, unless she counted some local politics on the front page of the *St. Louis Post-Dispatch.*

Suddenly, the headline in the local edition of the *National Tattler* caught her attention.

"Oh, my God." Lindy stepped out of line and went over to the newsstand. Her hand shook as she lifted the tabloid from the rack. "No. No," she whispered.

But her solemn plea remained unanswered. In large black letters, the *Tattler* screamed out to the entire St. Louis community the news that she was pregnant. The only saving grace was the fact that the paper didn't have a picture of her to go with the photograph of Shane and his parents.

"Are you in line?" Lindy turned to see a woman waiting beside her, coffee cup in hand. The stranger glanced at the tabloid. "Oh, he's cute. Hmm. Knocked up his PA. Lucky girl."

Lindy's hand shook. "Go ahead," she said. Paper in hand, Lindy stepped behind the woman.

"Do you want a bag?" the cashier asked Lindy.

"Y-Yes," Lindy stammered as the man proceeded to pack her purchases—a bottle of water, a banana, and a package of Hostess Ho Ho's, bought for the medicinal purpose of calming Lindy's nerves. The ensuing credit-card transaction took only a moment, and then Lindy found herself on autopilot, driving to Shane's.

Surely he hadn't seen the tabloid yet, she rationalized. But then again, there was a good chance that someone in his family had. The Jacobsens were notorious for having their public relations staff scour the press for any mention of the family that might be unsavory, and this article was front page.

As she pulled through the electronic gates, she knew she now had no choice. She had to talk about it. Hopefully she'd get to him before someone else did. Clutching her bag of goodies like a lifeline, Lindy stepped out of her car, opened the door to the pool house, and walked inside.

She knew immediately that he'd seen it. Maybe it was his posture. Maybe it was his way-too-casual attire. Maybe it was the seriousness of his expression. Whatever it was, his words confirmed her fears.

"Hello, Lindy," Shane said. "I think we need to talk, don't you?"

SHE'D SEEN the article. Shane knew this even before he saw the telltale newspaper sticking out of the brown paper sack. Lindy looked shell-shocked, and obvious guilt crossed her face. Once he'd thought she could never hide her feelings from him. Now he knew that Lindy had multiple layers, and that maybe he'd only seen a few of them.

She was late for work, and he'd spent the past half hour contemplating exactly what he wanted to say to her, what arguments, what chastisements.

But as her eyes brimmed with tears and her lips quivered, a rare feeling of possessiveness filled him, and all he wanted to do was to take her into his arms. Whether he was prepared for it, or liked it, this woman was the mother of his unborn child. They would be linked forever.

And he had to admit she was beautiful. Certainly she wasn't like the gorgeous women who had once adorned his arm, but Shane suddenly realized that Lindy had something those women would never have.

Lindy had inner beauty. She had class, an innate style that was all her own.

And even better, he liked her. Even now. Shane drew himself up. Yes, things could be much worse. If he had to be in this unfortunate situation, at least it was with Lindy.

"I know about the baby," he said quietly. Her brown eyes widened. "My mother called me first thing this morning to give me the third degree. Not quite a pleasant way to wake up, I assure you."

"I'm sorry," she whispered.

Shane bit his lower lip. "Did you ever plan on telling me?"

"I—"

"You didn't, did you?"

Lindy looked at her feet. "No."

"Aw hell, Lindy!"

Her refusal to tell him about the baby grated. "You just planned on running away, didn't you? No wonder your haste, your insistence on being professional only. Didn't you even want to ask about my health? You think I'm such a playboy, weren't you worried about whether you could have caught something else?"

Lindy didn't say anything.

"No answer? How about you, are you clean?"

Mortified, Lindy flushed bright red. "Yes! How dare you ask me that?"

"Dare? Easily. You've kept a lot from me. But at least you're okay." Shane took a moment to calm himself. "Anyway, you don't have to worry about me. I'm in excellent health, with a clean medical chart."

His voice was slightly bitter. "And, since I know about your pregnancy, what are we going to do about it?"

"I don't know," Lindy said. She lowered herself into a living-room chair.

Immediately, Shane was concerned. He had no experience with these things. Was she sick? "Are you okay?"

Lindy's hands shook as she pulled the bottled water out of the bag. "No. No, I'm not okay. Don't you understand? Nothing will ever be okay again. I didn't plan on this. I certainly didn't expect my life to be on the front page of the *National Tattler*."

"Actually, we're only there because of my parents," Shane said as he watched her take a sip of water. "In fact, we even made it onto CNN. I'm sure we'll be more fodder after my parents issue a statement."

Lindy's hand shook so much she almost spilt the water. "Oh, no."

He took no delight in her discomfort. "Oh, yes."

"Shane, I'm so sorry."

She was sorry. More words. Trying to find space to think, Shane paced the room. "I can tell you're sorry, Lindy, but that doesn't change the fact you kept all of this from me. I came to you and asked you who I'd been with. You lied to me, Lindy. You lied to me about that, and about being pregnant. You even lied about the real reason for quitting your job and going to Jacobsen."

"I didn't know I was pregnant when I accepted the job," Lindy said.

Shane shook his head. "It doesn't matter. All that matters right now is what we're going to do about it. And for once in my life, I'm going to do the right thing. You are going to marry me."

"I can't," Lindy said.

Shane stared at her. Had he heard her correctly? Surely she hadn't said… "What do you mean, you can't? You're having my baby!"

Lindy took a long sip of water and Shane watched her swallow. He'd never noticed the graceful curve of her neck before. Her brown eyes flicked toward him for a moment before she glanced away.

"Just because we're having a baby doesn't mean we have to get married," Lindy replied. "We don't love each other, Shane. A child needs parents who love each other, not parents who were forced together because birth control failed."

He felt his precarious control slip. Why was she being so difficult when the solution was so simple? "Look, Lindy, a child deserves two parents. I was raised by nannies. I know!"

"Shane, I understand your position, but no. I can't marry you and that's final." She was pleading for understanding without backing down. "We both live in the same town so we'll work out some sort of visitation schedule."

He stared at her in disbelief. "I never thought you could be so selfish."

Her lips quivered slightly. "I'm doing what's best

for the child. We would drive each other crazy if we were married. You know it, and I know it. We'd both wonder if we had missed that one great love of our life because we'd been trapped by circumstances. I can't marry you and allow you—I mean either of us— to lose that opportunity.''

Great love of his life? What was she talking about? Love was a fairy tale. ''This is a child we're talking about, not an opportunity. So what if we miss some great love. Isn't our child supposed to be that anyway?''

She raised her chin stubbornly. ''Perhaps. But once that child is grown and out of the house, then what? We'd be stuck with each other. We'd have grown apart during the years. We'd probably hate each other. Is that a solution? I don't think so.''

''I'm not having some other man being a stepfather to my child,'' Shane said. ''Absolutely not.''

''I don't like the idea of some other woman being a stepmother either,'' Lindy admitted.

''So we get married and eliminate that possibility,'' Shane declared. It was all so logical. Why couldn't Lindy just agree that doing the right thing was best for all of them, especially the baby? He had a sudden insight.

''If this is about your parents and their divorce, that won't happen to us,'' he promised. ''I know they're miles away and you hardly talk to them, but we won't hate each other like that. Ever. And I promise never to cheat on you.''

''That's all fine and good, but Shane, I don't want

to be like those couples who each have their separate interests because they're so unhappy at home. They don't cheat on their spouses, but they don't spend any time with them either. They're like roommates. I don't want that. When—rather if—I ever get married, I want to get married because I'm so in love with the person that he is my complementary better half."

That again. Good grief. He drew a frustrated hand through his hair. "Love is a silly idea that romance novelists make up so they can sell books. It doesn't exist, Lindy. It's a choice, not an emotion. If it was an emotion, I'd have found it."

"You don't have emotions," Lindy retorted.

Despite himself, Shane winced. Did she really think that badly of him? Her next words confirmed his fears.

"Seriously, I'm sure you don't like to hear this, but I really don't think you're capable of any deep, emotional feelings. It's simply not in you."

"Fine. Think what you want." Disconcerted by her outburst, Shane stopped pacing. "Look, Lindy, I'm trying to do the right thing here. I don't think that we'd be bad together. We've worked well together professionally. And we had phenomenal sex." He saw her look. "Oh yes, Lindy. I've got every bit of my memory back. I can tell you exactly what sounds you made when I did certain things to you."

"Enough," Lindy said. She tossed her hands in the air, causing water to splash out of the bottle she still clutched. "That doesn't matter, either. The answer is no, and it's staying no. I'm not marrying you and that's final. Tell your parents it's me that's refusing you. That should get you off the hook. Heck, I'll tell them if you want.''

''My parents aren't the reason I'm asking you to marry me. I want to marry you. I want our baby to have both parents.''

''The baby will, just not in the same household.''

Shane exhaled. When had she gotten so headstrong? Had he ever known her at all? ''That solution is not acceptable.''

''It will have to be.''

''I don't know why you're being so stubborn about this.''

''Me? Being stubborn? You're like a dog with a bone. You've got it in your mind that the only solution is to marry me and that's the way it's going to go.'' Lindy stood up. ''Well, let me tell you something, Shane Jacobsen, I'm a woman who can stand up to you. Your charm has never worked on me. I'm not marrying you and that's final. In fact, I don't even want to be here today. Or the rest of the week. If you don't mind, I can't stay here until Friday.''

''You're being childish, Lindy.''

''So sue me.'' And with that she walked to the door, threw it open and started. Grandpa Joe stood there, a concerned look on his face.

''Good morning, Lindy,'' he said. He looked past her and locked eyes with Shane. Shane groaned.

''Good morning,'' Lindy replied, and then with a curt ''Excuse me,'' she stepped past him. Seconds later, Shane heard her Grand Prix fire up and roar down the driveway.

"Another spat?" Grandpa Joe said as he walked in and shut the door behind him. He gave Shane a bemused smile. "And here I thought you had a way with the ladies."

"I'm not in the mood for jokes," Shane snapped. "And if you came to gloat, criticize or offer advice, don't bother. I've heard it all from my mother. I asked Lindy to marry me, and she said no."

As Grandpa Joe pursed his lips, his brow also furrowed. "I see."

"I'm sure you do. You have a way of seeing just about everything. What is that called? Clairvoyance? Precognition? Maybe you keep a tarot reader on speed dial?"

"It's called intuition," Grandpa Joe said. "And my guess is that your mother won't take this news about Lindy very well."

"I'm sure she already has the wedding planned, complete with the reporters in seats of honor so that the shine returns to Blake Jacobsen Ministries."

Shane reached out to inspect Lindy's bag of purchases, where the package of Ho Ho's and a banana lay forgotten. "Great. If this stuff is any indication, she didn't eat much this morning."

"So do you want to marry her?"

Did he? "I don't know. I just learned about this whole situation less than two hours ago. But yes, I know it's the right thing to do."

"Besides that, do you want to marry her? It's also the right thing for you to come and work at Jacobsen

Enterprises, but you've managed to avoid that responsibility so far.''

"This is different. There's a human being at stake here. A baby. Babies need two parents who will be there. Not like my parents who were always somewhere else. That's not going to happen to my son or daughter.''

Grandpa Joe shrugged. "Lindy wants to work. Her career is important to her. She's not going to be a stay-at-home mom unless she chooses to be.''

"So? I'm talking about single parenting, not staying at home. Let her have her career. I'm rich enough that neither of us has to work. If she wants, she can be the corporate hotshot and I can be a stay-at-home dad.''

Grandpa Joe's blue eyes narrowed. "You'd be okay with that?''

"Sure. Why not? No one thinks I work anyway.''

Grandpa Joe conceded that point with a nod of his head. "So, grandson, it seems to me that you have a small problem.''

Did everyone today have to state the obvious? "Tell me something I don't already know.''

"It's really simple, actually. If you want to marry Lindy, first you're going to have to woo her and win her.''

Shane blinked. Woo her? Win her? From what? "Uh, okay, but will you please explain why?''

"For someone who has a way with females, you are pretty clueless. Because Lindy's female. That means that like all females, she wants to marry for love. Not because she's pregnant and needs a father for her child. Lindy's a strong woman and she won't settle for less than true love. So for her to marry you, she'll need to fall in love with you.''

''So I'm supposed to *make* her fall in love with me?''

''She'll probably need to think that you're in love with her.''

''But I'm not in love with her,'' Shane retorted.

Grandpa Joe didn't blink. ''Pretend.''

Shane started pacing again. Lindy had just given him a huge lecture on love. Pretend? That's the last thing she'd want. ''That sounds underhanded.''

''Perhaps it is. But you have no other choice. I'm not going to fire her, and with a good job she doesn't need you. And despite your millions, the court system will leave your baby with his mother. Oh, I forgot to tell you. It will be a boy. The first of my great-grandchildren to carry on the Jacobsen name. Sure, you'll get visitation, but if you really want the baby *and* his mother, you'll have to woo Lindy.''

''Wonderful,'' Shane said. The idea really didn't sit well with him. It sounded like a ball and chain around both of their necks. ''So, really, I have no other choice?''

''No. Not if you want her to marry you.''

Shane sat and pondered Grandpa Joe's words. He'd never thought of Lindy in any sort of romantic sense before. But he had made love to her. His body stirred at that recollection, and he tamped down his immediate desire. Sex was not wooing. ''I have no idea how to proceed.''

Grandpa Joe smiled. "Of course you don't. You've always had women throw themselves at you. Well, I can give you some advice. After all, I won your grandmother and I did a mighty fine job of it, if I do say so myself."

"That was over fifty years ago," Shane interrupted.

"So? Winning with women is a timeless art, boy. In the past, you've just enjoyed the chase. Once you got them, you didn't want them anymore. Well, the chase isn't what it's about. That's lesson number one."

"And lesson number two?"

Grandpa Joe came and sat down by Shane. "Listen to your elders. Lindy's coming to work at Jacobsen Enterprises. So are you."

"But I said—"

Grandpa Joe's look silenced Shane. "Lesson three. Show her you're marriage material. Show her you're responsible. Lesson four. Show her you've changed. You can do all of that by coming to work for me."

A sinking feeling crept into Shane's stomach as Grandpa Joe continued. "And being family, you'll get a great spot as a vice president. Almost on a par with Harry. After all, he has worked for Jacobsen longer, so it's only fair that he's a smidge higher on the totem pole than you. Regardless, you'll start tomorrow."

Shane made one last attempt to hold on to his fast-disappearing freedom. "I don't like it and I don't see what this has to do with wooing Lindy."

"Let's see. Office co-workers. Office romances. Sure, they get a little sticky sometimes, but there are a lot of really nice single men working for Jacobsen. Lindy might meet someone and…''

A raw jealousy shot through Shane. ''That's not going to happen.''

''So then, make sure it doesn't happen. Be where she is. It's your only choice,'' Grandpa Joe said. ''That is, unless you can think of another one?''

Shane rubbed a hand over his jaw. He'd been had. Signed, sealed, delivered…and had. Grandpa Joe had finally gotten his way and trapped Shane into joining Jacobsen Enterprises. But was it for the best? Shane tried to rally his spirits. After he married Lindy, he could always be a stay-at-home dad. There, that cheered him up. ''No, you're right. I can't think of another way.''

Grandpa Joe smiled. ''Then I'll see you at headquarters first thing tomorrow.''

''But Lindy…''

''Trust me, I overheard it all. She won't be coming back to the Shane Jacobsen Foundation. And she doesn't start with me for a week and a half. You need to be there tomorrow. Get settled in. And out of the goodness of my heart, I'll even give you a corner office. I've been holding it for you for a while now. It was my next enticement.''

Resignation overcame Shane. ''You always get your way, don't you?''

''Yes,'' Grandpa Joe said. ''But my way is the right way. And Shane, I promise you that everything will turn out just fine in the end. You'll see.''

"I've heard that before. My father says that all the time."

"Ah, but Blake's not me. He's more like Henrietta. You're more like me. Trust me."

"I have no other choice."

Grandpa Joe's blue eyes twinkled. "No, you don't. Welcome aboard, grandson. Oh, and this little secret about your employment, we'll keep that to ourselves for a while. We don't want Lindy to get word of it. Not yet. Let it be, well, a surprise."

Chapter Five

"And this is your new home-away-from-home," the bubbly personnel worker enthused. She stopped outside a nondescript gray cubicle on the nineteenth floor. A small placard on the outside partition displayed Lindy's name.

"Thanks," Lindy said. She stepped inside, set her purse down on the smooth laminated surface and glanced around the cubicle. Her new home was not quite nine feet by nine feet, but it contained an L-shaped desk, a rolling desk chair, a computer, a small bookcase, and a circular two-person worktable complete with two burgundy-colored plastic chairs. Definitely a far cry from the more spacious accommodations that she and Shane had shared.

She pushed thoughts of Shane out of her mind. Ever since that fateful morning when she'd walked out, Lindy had been trying to erase Shane from her mind. More often than not, she failed miserably. Little things would remind her of the fun times they'd shared over the three years they'd worked together, and once, in the library, she'd seen a little boy with hair almost the same color as Shane's. And the memory of that morning, and the way Shane had looked at her...

Attempting to erase the image, she shook her head so forcefully that the personnel assistant asked, "Are you okay?"

Lindy smiled to mask her goof. No matter what, she had to focus on the matter at hand. She was finally at Jacobsen, and after being in introductory and training meetings all morning, she was not going to let the memory of Shane ruin her first afternoon in her new job. "Yes. I'm okay. Just something in my eye."

"Oh, okay. Well, here, as promised, are the files that you'll need to get started." With a well-manicured fingernail, the personnel assistant tapped a stack of folders that sat on the worktop. "Any other questions?"

Lindy glanced at her own hands. As usual, her short nails were bare of polish. "No," she replied.

"Great. Well, once again, welcome to Jacobsen Enterprises. If you think of any other questions later, don't hesitate to call me. I'm at extension four-o-five."

"Thanks," Lindy said, and with that the assistant departed, and Lindy found herself alone.

She looked around again, taking in the soothing neutral colors. For the first time in a long while, she was finally on her own. No one else in charge of her world but her. Lindy's knees weakened slightly, so she sat down in the desk chair located by the computer. She adjusted her skirt and took another quick glance around the cubicle. It needed pictures and personalization. She'd do that slowly. She reached for a folder. Time to begin work.

Four hours later Lindy placed the same folder back onto the top of the stack. So much for being alone, not that she'd minded. She hadn't gotten much accomplished because most of her new co-workers had stopped by to scope her out, offer advice, and generally just welcome her to the job.

Shelby Gantly poked her head inside Lindy's cubicle. Lindy had immediately liked the young girl, who was fresh out of college. "Hey, a group of us are going to happy hour at the Tap Room. We'd love it if you would join us."

Although she couldn't drink any of the Tap Room's famous ale, Lindy took a moment to consider. It was, after all, an opportunity to make friends and socialize with her new colleagues.

"Whoa," Shelby said softly. She placed a hand on her collarbone and craned her neck to get a better look down the aisle. "What's *he* doing on this floor?"

"Who?" Lindy said. She tried to see exactly what Shelby was looking at, but with her co-worker in the cubicle entrance, Lindy couldn't see anything.

Shelby's hand fluttered a little, and she looked both excited and apprehensive. "I don't believe it. He's coming this way!"

"Who?"

But Shelby didn't answer Lindy's question. Instead she said, "Hello, Mr. Jacobsen."

Lindy relaxed a little. Now Shelby's behavior made sense. It was just Grandpa Joe. He'd told her he would check up on her, and Grandpa Joe was known for roaming the company and surprising people. "Hello, Mr. Jacobsen," Lindy said.

"Hello," Shane Jacobsen replied.

As the warm, familiar baritone of Shane's voice washed over her, Lindy bolted upright in her chair. Shelby moved aside as Shane stepped into the small entryway.

"Shane! What are you doing here?"

"Checking up on you." He eased himself into one of the plastic chairs and slid his legs under the small table.

He smiled then, the million-dollar smile that melted women's hearts for miles. It was working on Shelby, for she seemed star-struck. "Miss Gantly, would you mind excusing us? Lindy was my PA, and I'd love to have a private word."

"Oh. Of course." Shelby backed up, her eyes blinking rapidly as comprehension set in. She glanced back and forth from Lindy's stomach to Shane's face. Lindy inwardly groaned. She knew Shelby had just put two and two together, added baby, and come up with five.

This was not exactly the way that Lindy had wanted to start her new job at Jacobsen, being known as Shane Jacobsen's former PA and, obviously, the one he'd knocked up.

"We'll be at the Tap Room. Join us if you want. You, too, Mr. Jacobsen," Shelby added for good measure before retreating.

Shane pinched an imaginary piece of lint off his suit coat sleeve and again turned on that high-watt smile, this time for Lindy's benefit. "So, tell me, Lindy, how was your day?"

"Fine," Lindy said. She placed her hands in her lap. Despite herself, she couldn't help but stare at him and drink in his presence, like a person who finds water in the desert.

Shane looked magnificent.

Of course, he always did, but now, in the suit she knew to be custom Armani, he'd never looked better. He'd had his hair cut in a more fashionable and flattering style, making him look dignified, like one of those guys on the cover of *GQ* or *Forbes*. He'd exchanged the traditional white shirt for a designer-blue number, and his tie, Lindy knew, had cost a small fortune.

His blue eyes twinkled. "All you're going to tell me is that your day was fine?"

"It was fine," Lindy said.

He gave her a knowing nod. "Ah, I see I've rendered you speechless."

"In your dreams," Lindy retorted, angry with herself for being affected by his presence in the small space.

His next words didn't help, and neither did the smug smile crossing his face. "Oh, believe me, you've been in my dreams. So how have you been?"

She rallied her defenses. She could not let him waltz right back into her life and under her skin. "I've been fine," Lindy replied.

"Just fine," Shane mused. "Is that the only word you know? Fine?"

"Yes, fine." Lindy drew herself up. "Shane, we've always cut to the chase. Why are you here?"

"To see how your first day went," he replied. He made himself even more comfortable, adding to her tension.

"Really. You're telling me that you got all dressed up and drove down here just to check up on me. I find that hard to believe. You hate this place."

"Nah," Shane said with a relaxed shrug of his shoulders. He placed his hands behind his head. "I just thought I did. No Lindy, you're looking at a re-formed man. I've even got an office upstairs. You'll have to come up and see it sometime. Right down the hall from Harry's and around the corner from my uncle's."

Lindy's jaw dropped open. "April Fool's Day was over two months ago, Shane. Try again."

He didn't look repentant. "Why? It's the truth. I'm a vice president. Of course, I am a bit lower on the ladder than Harry, but I'm above Megan."

Lindy's hands shook in her lap, and she clenched them together more tightly. "No!"

"Yes. I started the day after you walked out. Why not? After all, I never really did work. And you know, real work feels rather good. I hate to admit it, but my grandfather was right. I just finally took him up on his idea."

"You're not working here!"

His tone turned serious. He lowered his hands. "Uh, yes I am. After all, it *is* my family company."

"You *can't* work here."

"I just explained it to you."

"No!" Lindy was almost shouting. Her world was crumbling. Shane couldn't. He wouldn't. But he had. "You can't. I came here to get away from you."

Shane shrugged and gave her a bittersweet look as if he understood and sympathized with her pain, but wasn't about to change. Not until he got what he wanted. "I'm sorry, Lindy, but you're carrying my baby. I'm not letting you get away. I'm not going to let that happen."

"It has to happen," Lindy whispered. Unresolved fear churned in her stomach. Didn't he understand? He would never love her. She couldn't live the rest of her life with him, and not be loved. She tried again to reason with him. "I understand what you're saying, but it won't work between us. It has to be this way, Shane."

He shifted his posture, now pure business. "No, it doesn't. We need to work together, Lindy, for the sake of the baby. I'm here, and since you won't marry me, I'm going to watch over you. I care about you enough to do that. You know me, so I know you understand that I have to do at least that much."

Lindy's chin jutted forward stubbornly. "I can take care of myself."

Shane reached forward, covering her hands with his own. A raw and immediate longing burned through her, but even as she tried to pull away he simply held on tighter, as if he knew he could weaken her resolve. Those baby blues of his blinked only once as they gazed into her eyes.

"I know you can take care of yourself, Lindy," he said. "That's always been one of the things that I've admired about you. You're so strong. You're a survivor. But you're no longer alone. You have me."

But she really didn't have him, and that was the problem. Shane had grabbed onto her like a new toy, or like a line to salvation. He'd found in Lindy's pregnancy a purpose, perhaps even a reason to reform. But deep down, she knew he hadn't changed. He was, and ever would be, a playboy. She pictured him hanging out late at night at the country-club bar with all the rest of the disillusioned husbands—men who would never cheat on their wives, but would never truly love them enough to be partners in every sense of the word.

She didn't want that. She had to hold out for love. No matter what, she was not going to settle for second best.

"I have to go home now," she said.

"No happy hour?" Shane asked with a lift of his blond eyebrow.

"No."

"So can I interest you in dinner, instead?"

Lindy shook her head. "I don't think so."

To her surprise, Shane didn't protest. He simply removed his hands from hers, and instantly she missed their warmth.

"Maybe another time," he said. "After all, we're working together again."

"That we are," Lindy replied. She stood up, placed her hands on her lower back and stretched. Although she wasn't showing at all, she was beginning to ex-

perience the aches and pains of adding extra pounds
to her five-foot-seven-inch figure.

Shane watched her like a hawk. Lindy appreciated
that he didn't ask her any more questions she didn't
want to, or couldn't, answer. He stepped out into the
now-empty corridor between the many cubicles. "I'll
see you around," Lindy said.

"Plan on it," Shane answered.

"SO HOW DID IT GO?"

Shane whirled around. His grandfather seemed able
to pop up everywhere. Shane knew Grandpa Joe
hadn't been standing in the empty corridor by Lindy's
cubicle for very long, just long enough to let Lindy
leave by herself.

"I guess it went fine," Shane replied.

Grandpa Joe's white eyebrow arched. "Fine?"

Frustration built up inside Shane. "She didn't look
to happy to see me, that's for sure. She told me it
would be better if we didn't see each other."

"Par for the course," Grandpa Joe said.

"Par for the course?" Shane repeated as his frustration mounted. "Your plan didn't work. I even asked
her to dinner. She resisted everything."

Grandpa Joe grinned. "Of course she did. She's not
like your other bimbos. She's got integrity. That's why
you like her. Heck, that's why I like her. Unlike your
other featherweights, she's not a pushover. You'll just
have to keep working on her."

"There's that work word again."

"Exactly. Work. I know it's still a bit of a foreign

word in your vocabulary, but you're learning. Remember those steps I told you about. Lesson two, listen to your elders. Lesson four, show her you've changed. Did you think it would be overnight? Women are like fine wine. They take a bit of time to mellow. Anyway, I need to speak with you about the Jonnsburger project. Do you have a moment?''

Shane looked toward the elevator doors. Lindy was gone, her sentiments toward marrying him still unchanged. And he really didn't want to meet his friends for happy hour.

''I have all the time in the world,'' Shane told his grandfather.

''Good,'' Grandpa Joe said, his double meaning clear.

IT WASN'T UNTIL Lindy reached the safety of her apartment that she allowed herself to breathe normally. She'd half expected Shane to follow her, and still didn't know if she was relieved or disappointed that he hadn't.

''So how was your first day at work?'' Tina came out of the bathroom, a big white towel on her hair.

Lindy found herself using that F-word again. ''Fine.''

''Fine?'' Tina adjusted the strap on her robe. ''You look a little too pale for it to have been fine. What happened?''

Lindy hesitated for a quick second, but then her need for her best friend's reassurance won. ''Shane's working at Jacobsen and everyone on my floor now knows I'm the girl he knocked up.''

Tina scowled. ''Not a good way to start.''

''No.'' Lindy put her feet up on the coffee table. Even though she hadn't been standing much during the day, her feet hurt. Was she swelling up already? She looked at the end table. ''Where's my pregnancy book?''

''That what to expect one? I hid it,'' Tina said.

''Hid it?''

''Yeah. You've been such a hypochondriac lately, thinking that you've had fifty things wrong with you, so my mother suggested I just take it from you. So I did.''

''Give it back.''

''No. Not until you admit what's really wrong.'' Tina took the towel off her hair and dropped it onto the floor. She fingered out her hair.

Lindy made a grumpy face. ''Since you're so all-wise, why don't you tell me what's wrong?''

''You're missing Shane.''

An exasperated noise escaped Lindy's pursed lips. ''I am not missing Shane.''

Tina stopped working her fingers through her hair. ''Lindy, he's the father of your child and the man you're in love with. Break down and admit that you two belong together.''

''He doesn't love me.''

''So? I mean, I personally can't stand the man, but it's starting to get where I can't stand you, and you know how much I love you. Lindy, he's a part of you now, and no matter what, you must do what's best for your baby.''

"Marrying Shane is not what's best for my baby."

Tina smiled wryly. "Well, I tried."

Lindy looked at her suspiciously. "Tried what? What's going on?"

"You've got a message on the answering machine and I'm going out." With that announcement, Tina picked up her towel and headed to the bathroom.

Lindy leaned her head back on the sofa and closed her eyes. *Shane had called!* In a perverse way, she was pleased. She really should check the answering machine. Instead, she closed her eyes.

The insistent ringing of the doorbell shattered whatever dream Lindy had been having. A quick glance at the clock told her she'd only been dozing about twenty minutes. "Tina, your date's here," she called.

Tina appeared, dressed in a stylish black shirt, black flats, and a pair of black shorts. "I don't have a date," she said as she grabbed her purse. "I'm meeting Jane for a movie."

"Oh," Lindy said. She turned her head so she would be able to see Jane when Tina opened the door. But it wasn't Jane that walked in.

"Hello, Lindy. You did get the message I was coming over, didn't you?"

As Lindy scrambled to her feet, Tina shot her a "sorry" look as she stepped out the door without saying a word.

"Mrs. Jacobsen."

"Call me Sara," Sara Jacobsen said as she swooped

into the apartment. Her presence made the room seem smaller. "After all, friends don't call each other by their last names, now do they?"

"No," Lindy admitted. She eyed Sara. As usual, Shane's mother was dressed impeccably, this time in a beige pantsuit. Although she was not wearing one stitch of designer wear—even though she could well afford it—the maven of Blake Jacobsen Ministries had refined the art of discount chic.

Like money that could be better spent elsewhere, Sara also never wasted time. "Lindy, we have to talk."

Five dreaded words. "Okay," Lindy said slowly.

Sara got directly to the point. "Lindy, you must marry Shane. I know you've already said no, so before I give you my reasons, I want you to give me yours. Please, give me at least one good reason why you will not marry my son, the father of your baby."

Lindy looked at Shane's mother. Sara's brown eyes remained unblinking as she stared back. Lindy took a deep breath. "He doesn't love me," she replied.

Sara shook her head. "Not good enough."

Lindy opened her mouth to protest, but Sara wasn't about to be stopped now. She held her hand up. "Let me finish. I know he doesn't love you. I know you know it, too. But Lindy, there are times when we must do things we don't want to do because of the cause. In your case, because of the precious innocent life that is at stake."

Sara paused to draw a quick breath. "I've known you for what, almost three years?"

Lindy nodded.

"Exactly. You're a young professional female with visions of romance dancing in your head. You want the man to buy you flowers, profess undying gratitude and endless infatuation. You want him to grovel. It won't happen. Life is not a soap opera. All that frilly stuff is media hype to help businesses make money." Sara leaned forward. "Love is a choice and a feeling, Lindy. And if you love your baby, you'll do the right thing and marry its father."

"Marriage is antiquated," Lindy said. "Children are born to single parents all the time in this modern day and age."

"Perhaps," Sara said, "and yes, God could have had Jesus born to a single Mary instead of arranging a marriage to Joseph. But he didn't now, did he?"

Sara paused to let that point sink in a little. "Lindy, you aren't having an ordinary baby now, are you? You're having a Jacobsen. This baby's grandfather is a world leader. Yes, your decision is personal to us because it embarrasses us greatly. But as adults we have the strength to deal with that trial in our lives. But an innocent baby should not have to deal with it at all."

"I'm not planning on having my baby in the limelight," Lindy said. She shifted a little bit, folding her legs so that she could curl her feet up underneath her. Her voice rose slightly with her next words. "Does no one seem to understand that? I plan on protecting my child from parents who don't love each other. You may not know that I had a horrible childhood. My parents were always fighting. When they weren't avoiding each other, they threw things at each other. Shane doesn't love me, and I will not have my child raised in a house where the parents don't love each other. It's not fair to the baby. And don't give me that social stigmatism about being out-of-wedlock. No one cares these days.''

''Actually, they do.'' Sara reached into a beige purse that matched the color of her pantsuit and drew out several newspaper clippings. She handed them to Lindy, and Lindy's hand trembled as she saw them. ''In some parts of the world, Lindy, people care very much.''

The headlines of various American and world newspapers jumped out her. One tabloid had dubbed her the ''single sinner.'' Another had made up a story about how she seduced Shane and tossed him aside, that she'd only used him because her biological clock was ticking. A more conservative religious paper's editorial went so far as to damn her to hell.

''Because we are international figures, and you're having our son's child, *you* are now an international figure, Lindy. Do you want your son or daughter to grow up with the media speculating about all these goings-on? How will you explain to your son or daughter that Daddy wanted to marry you and be a family under one roof, but you said no? Can you answer that, Lindy?''

And Lindy couldn't. She handed the tabloid articles back and instead took the only path she knew might relieve her guilt. She went on the offensive.

"Sara, look, perhaps you failed with Shane. After all, he's a disgrace to you and to Blake. He's named one of the world's top playboys on a yearly basis. He hits the eligible bachelor lists. He sees too many women and sows too many oats. But you cannot save him, or your reputation, through my child or me. Shane is Shane. And as for being a good parent, do you think you have the right to lecture me on what makes a good parent?"

Lindy's chest heaved, and she drew a quick breath. "Yes, you and Blake love each other and have a wonderful partnership. But you let nannies raise Shane while you were gallivanting all over the world. He's closer to the family cook than he is to you. You and Blake didn't even remember to call him on his twenty-fifth birthday because you were so busy in Australia. In fact, if you had remembered to call him in the first place, he wouldn't have felt sorry for himself, had a party, and gotten into bed with me. So don't you lecture me. I think if Grandpa Joe weren't holding this family together, Shane wouldn't even ever see you. So in a nutshell, I don't think you have any room to talk about my choices."

Sara looked stricken. Silence descended on the room, and Sara used the time to put the clippings back into her purse. Finally, she looked up at Lindy. "Perhaps part of what you say is true. Perhaps Blake and I haven't been good parents. I freely admit that we have made mistakes that we'd both love to undo. But we can't turn back time, as you well know. Perhaps your parents weren't too good either. So, yes, you and

Shane have two strikes against you. But there's such a thing as still being able to hit a home run even when the count is against you. You and Shane have the benefit of your experiences in what not to do. But no matter what, the right thing to do is not to set your child up to fail from birth. Blake and I tried to keep Shane out of the limelight, and you've just told me in no uncertain terms how well our plan to protect him backfired. So why don't you think about your plan, Lindy? The media is already onto this baby's existence. He or she is already marked for life. You won't be able to protect this baby, no matter how hard you try. The least you can do is provide the child with a happy home.''

Sara stood up. ''And lastly, you've been one of the best things to ever happen to Shane. You two probably have a better chance for happiness than most of the people that I've met in this world. If you don't think that he loves you in some way, then you're the sorriest fool I've ever met.''

And with that, Sara left without another word or a goodbye, the door ominously clicking closed behind her.

Lindy stared at the door that still needed a fresh coat of paint. As the only sound in the room became the faint click of the clock, Lindy wondered if Sara had actually been there at all. She stood up, locked the door, and walked into the kitchen to get herself a glass of water. Her brain was still reeling from the conversation.

Shane loving her even a little? Of course he did. He

loved that she was convenient. That she organized his schedule. That she dumped his women for him with unparalleled efficiency. That's what he loved about her. But he didn't love *her*. And that was the difference.

For a moment she thought of Craig, and wondered what ever happened to him. He'd been such a nice guy and he'd been crazy for her. They'd had a few odd dates here and there, but she'd never really been able to get into him because of her obsession with Shane. For that's what it was, she'd decided. Not love. Obsession.

"Ah, you're kidding yourself again," Lindy said out loud as she reached for an apple. Before she could take a bite, someone knocked on her door. "Great," Lindy said. After all, nothing about the day had been ordinary, and it sure couldn't get any worse.

Expecting Sara once again, Lindy instead found Shane on her doorstep. She drew back from the peephole. After the fun visit with Sara, should she pretend she wasn't home?

No such luck. "I know you're in there," Shane said. "I just got the phone call from my mother saying she was leaving. From the tone of her voice, I figured she wasn't very kind. So I brought a peace offering." Lindy glanced out the peephole again and saw Shane holding up some familiar black-and-white paper bags. "Now come on, Lindy. Stop hanging out on the other side of the door and let me in."

"Only because you brought food," she called before opening the door. Shane stepped in, bringing with him the aroma of hamburgers. "I admit, I can't resist. You brought Steak 'n Shake."

Shane's playboy grin melted into a delicious smile. "Yep. I got you a Frisco melt, large fries and a chocolate shake. Your absolute to-die-for-favorites, besides Hostess Ho Ho's. Those, I regret, I don't have. As for me, I'm having chili."

Shane set the food on the coffee table, and Lindy noticed he had changed. Now, instead of a business suit, he wore a pair of chino shorts and a polo shirt. She tried not to stare at his legs, already slightly tanned from the hours Shane spent out on the golf course. She swallowed, trying to focus on the food.

"Anyway," Shane said, "when I got home from work, there was a message on the answering machine from my mother saying that she was going to pay you a visit. So as soon as I changed my clothes, I got in the car and headed over. Sorry I didn't make it in time to stop her. When she called me again after leaving here, I figured your favorite fast food was in order. So tell me, did she get you good?"

"I think I gave back just as well," Lindy admitted.

"Good for you." Shane sat down and began unloading the bags. Lindy watched him pull a Frisco melt out of a white paperboard box. "I had no idea she was planning a stunt like this. My apologies. You haven't eaten dinner yet, have you?"

Lindy thought of her apple. "No."

"Didn't think so. It's nearly seven. You should have eaten."

"I was getting around to it. But Steak 'n Shake

burgers definitely win.'' Lindy came and sat down in the chair perpendicular to the couch. Shane had opened her food box and poured her large French fries into the lid. Now he was busy ripping open the small ketchup packets. Lindy had to admit, everything looked wonderful, including him.

The lights highlighted the golden hairs on his arms and legs, and a cowlick on the top of his head was trying to work its way free from the new corporate haircut. Lindy sighed. Would she ever be able to see him and not long for him? Making an effort to take her mind off Shane, she reached for the chocolate shake, put in the straw, and took a long, deep pull.

When the ice cream and milk concoction hit her tongue, Lindy closed her eyes. As always, the taste was absolute heaven. She sipped for a while, ignoring the small knot forming between her eyebrows. A cold headache was a welcome side effect, part of the plea-sure of drinking a real chocolate milkshake. She opened her eyes to find Shane staring at her. ''What?''

He seemed a bit flustered, for he still held a partially opened ketchup packet between his thumbs and fore-fingers. He shook his head as if trying to clear it. ''Nothing,'' he said.

''Tell me,'' Lindy said, for she knew Shane, and when he said nothing it always meant something. Right now, she knew he was lying. ''Tell me,'' she repeated.

''No, I better not.''

''Tell me,'' Lindy repeated, a bit more forcefully this time.

Once again Shane shook his head, and he made a show of squeezing the ketchup into her steakburger box lid.

"I want to know," Lindy said.

Shane shook his head again and took the plastic lid off the bowl of what Steak 'n Shake called Chili Deluxe. Steam wafted up. "I'm not sure you do want to know. I'm not sure I even want to tell you."

"Well, I'm sure. Tell me."

"You didn't tell me about your day," he argued.

"That was different. Tell me."

Shane's blue eyes clouded slightly before he turned to reach for a package of oyster crackers, which he stirred into the steaming brown chili. The melting cheddar and Monterey Jack cheeses formed ribbons between the crackers. Finally he glanced at Lindy, and his gaze locked onto hers. "When you closed your eyes it reminded me of how you looked when we were in bed. Like when I was inside you."

Okay. Maybe she hadn't wanted to know that. She turned to hide her own eyes as, immediately, the image of their lovemaking jumped into her brain. She could still feel the smooth of his skin, smell the musky scent that was so simply him. She remembered how those beautiful blue eyes darkened into deep pools that she swam in each time she crested. Just now, Lindy realized, he'd watched her close her eyes, suck on a straw, and thought of their lovemaking.

Not knowing how to respond to Shane's revelation, she took a bite of the Frisco melt. Although the taste and feel of the food in her mouth was comforting,

Lindy made sure not to close her eyes this time. She and Shane fell into an awkward silence. "Do you want to watch TV?" Lindy asked.

"Sure," Shane said. Lindy found a channel showing a popular late-1980s sitcom.

Fifteen minutes later, Shane pushed aside his empty bowl. "My mother didn't give you too much trouble, did she?"

"No."

Shane looked relieved. "Good. I told her to stay out of this, but you know my mother. She couldn't stay out of a situation like this to save her life. So did she succeed?"

"In what?"

"Browbeating you into marrying me."

Lindy smiled. "Sorry, but no."

Shane broke into a wide smile. "Didn't think so. But she was determined to try."

"I think that's what mothers do," Lindy said. "I'm sure I'll be that way, you know, trying to smooth over problems and riding to the rescue when I perceive my child to be in danger."

Shane's expression sobered. "I bet you will. You'll be great at motherhood, Lindy. And if I haven't said it, I think I'm lucky that you're the mother of my child. My child couldn't have a better mother."

Deep words from Shane were unheard-of, totally unfamiliar territory, and Lindy tried to make light of the moment. "You're just trying to soften me up, get under my skin so that I'll marry you."

Shane's expression turned even more serious. "No,

I'm not. When you've said no, you mean no. Believe me, I've learned that lesson. After all, you're not working for me now, are you?''

"Well, technically, I am. You're somehow my superior at Jacobsen.''

He grinned. "Okay, I am right behind Harry on the chain of command. But you know what I meant. I was talking about when I worked out of my home. Speaking of which, I'm moving out.''

"You're what?''

"Moving out. The pool house isn't a real home, and when my son or daughter comes to stay with me, I want him or her to have a real house. A real place to be. I'm looking for property. The Ladue and Clayton school districts are good, so I'm concentrating on those. Of course, my parents believe that junior should have a private-school education, but, I mean, for grade school? But I figure we have a few years to decide that. Anyway, Ladue and Clayton are close to Jacobsen Enterprises. I don't want too much of a commute.''

Shane's face brightened as if he'd been struck by a great idea. "You know, you should probably come look at houses with me. After all, you might want to give the place a seal of approval.''

"I'm not sure," Lindy said. The prospect of looking for houses with Shane was, well, overwhelming. How often had she fantasized about that?

"I think you should," Shane said. "I mean, I might get this totally modern thing that is nowhere near, what's that word, kidproof. And I'm buying a new car.''

''You're giving up your Corvette?''

Shane looked sheepish. ''I didn't say that. I mean, it's a fiftieth anniversary edition. I'm buying a second car. A sensible sedan with a back seat where I can strap in a baby carrier. I'm torn between two models, a Lexus or a Buick. Both have excellent safety ratings. Hey, how about I get the brochures? They're in my car.''

''Well, I—''

''It'll only take a minute,'' Shane said. He scrambled to his feet and was out the door before she could protest further.

Once again, Lindy found herself staring at the door. Tomorrow she resolved to call the apartment complex and have them paint it. A few moments later, she heard Shane's footsteps on the landing, and then he entered. ''Got them,'' he announced. ''Here, look at these. Say, it's Monday night. Want to go for a test drive with me? The dealership's open until nine.''

Lindy thought of her Grand Prix. Three years ago she'd splurged on the top-of-the-line model because car payments and rent were her only two big monthly expenses. Now Shane was showing her brochures for cars that cost twice as much as her GTP. Once again she said the words that were all too familiar where Shane was concerned. ''I'm not sure that's a good idea.''

''Sure it is,'' Shane said. ''Be impulsive for once.

You're finished eating, and television's boring. Let's go.''

"Really, I…''

"Come on.'' Shane pulled her to her feet, and in the process Lindy found herself falling against him. As her body pressed his, fire seared her and her body fully betrayed her as her nipples thrust forward, seeking closer contact with Shane's chest. Lindy's face flushed as she realized that heat had traveled even farther south.

"Steady, there,'' Shane said, and he encircled her in his arms. "I've got you.''

He did, too, and Lindy's face reddened again as she realized that she wasn't the only one slightly aroused. That she could cause such a reaction in Shane, when he wasn't drunk, surprised her. She lifted her head to look at him.

Which was a mistake.

Those baby-blue Jacobsen eyes had morphed into bottomless pools she could easily drown in. Those lips of Shane's were way too close. She could feel his warm breath on her cheek, feel the soft hairs of his arms underneath her fingertips.

She could feel how much he wanted her.

Her. Lindy Brinks. Former PA.

"Speechless,'' Shane mused, and then as if fate had finally decided, he swooped his lips down.

Chapter Six

The moment his lips touched hers, Lindy shattered. The fact that he didn't pull away caused her to detonate.

How long had it been? Eight weeks? Ten? Right now she couldn't remember the exact length of time since their last kiss, but as Shane touched his lips lightly to hers again, Lindy didn't care.

Shane was kissing her.

Wait. *Shane was kissing her.* The insistent little voice inside her head tried to intrude, but as Shane ran his wet tongue over the outside of her lips, Lindy banished the nagging voice of reason to the deepest netherworld region of her brain.

The first time they'd ever kissed he'd been under the influence of painkillers and strawberry daiquiris. This time, as he kissed her, he tasted of chili and cheese mixed with cola. He tasted delicious. Delightful. Divine.

"Kiss me," he whispered against her lips, and upon hearing those two words Lindy's final resistance caved. She pressed her lips back to his. His fingers

traced her jaw as his lips feathered over hers, beck-
oning her to take another taste, to deepen the intimacy
of their mating mouths.

"Kiss me," she whispered back, before parting his
lips with a quick darting tongue movement of her own.

"I will," Shane said, and as the words traveled the
millimeters from his mouth to hers, Shane knew he
would kiss her. Forever if he could. Her mouth tasted
of chocolate and of French fries, and right now no
caviar or champagne could be richer or tastier. As he
kissed her, he realized that he'd lost all control. Kissing her was like discovering an awe-inspiring power,
an electrical storm that could heat and cool the entire
world. But along with this raging passion, there was
still a simple beauty, a glorious grace to Lindy that
made kissing her special, different from any other kiss
he'd ever had before.

Shane slid his arms lower around her waist, bringing
her hips toward his. He wanted to feel her close again.
To remember. To relive what they'd shared. He deepened the kiss, devouring her mouth as if he'd been
seeking its fruit his whole life. His veins felt molten,
and his knees weak. No other woman had ever done
that to him. He reached up with one hand and threaded
his fingers into her hair. Just as silky and smooth as
he'd semiremembered it being, had subsequently fantasized it being.

He knew at that moment he should probably stop
the kiss, but in a split second he decided not to. If he
stopped her before she wanted to, guilt might sink in.
He didn't want that, not when everything in her body

language told him to go on. No, he'd move slowly, giving her all opportunities.

He moved her slightly, knocking the car brochures off of the table and down to the floor. She didn't seem to notice or care. He lowered her to the couch, and she only moved her lips to change the angle of her kiss.

Part of him raged to simply take her into the bedroom and ravish her. But this was Lindy, and this time he wanted it to be slow. He wanted to savor her. He wanted to taste every bit of her skin as he slid his lips lower, feeling with his fingertips every bit of phenomenal friction as his hands experienced the texture of her skin.

He mated his tongue with hers, and Lindy's hands suddenly laced themselves into his hair. The feeling of her touch ricocheted through him and his lower body quickened further. Realizing his eyes were closed, he drew back a moment and opened his eyes. In doing so, he saw that Lindy was staring up at him, the most intense look on her face. Her brown-eyed gaze held his as her hands, still in his hair, pulled him back down for another long kiss.

Was this what it had been like before? Shane tried to remember, but when his hands slid underneath Lindy's broadcloth shirt and found her lace bra, his mind blanked as the new history overwrote the old. She arched her back up into him, and Shane could deny himself no longer. He kissed her neck, laved the skin revealed at the V-neckline of her blouse, and then, instead of unbuttoning the bothersome article of clothing, he simply yanked the shirt up and kissed Lindy through the white lace.

She wore white lace. Surprise ripped through him, although somehow he should have known that Lindy would be a white-lace type of girl. Did she know how much he loved white lace? How much it turned him on, and how Lindy in white lace was the biggest turn-on he'd ever had?

He'd have to tell her later, he resolved, and his mind lost focus and drifted off again into fields of pleasure as his teeth nibbled, his mouth suckled, and underneath him Lindy went positively wild as pleasure and abandon racked her body.

"That's right, let go," he whispered as he moved his kisses to her other straining breast. He lowered his mouth to it, and with deft fingers began undoing the buttons of Lindy's skirt. She hadn't changed out of her work clothes, but he didn't want a quick coupling with her skirt shoved up at her waist. No, he wanted her bare as the day she was born. He wanted nothing on her but the sheen of her skin.

She arched her head back, and Shane knew that even if she stopped him after his next action, he'd have at least broken down some of the barriers she'd put up around herself in these past few weeks. With a fast swoop he slid her skirt off, and he went mad. Lindy had always maintained that she hated panty hose. He'd never understood or paid much attention, until now. Instead of waist-high hose, she wore individual thigh-highs. And covering her most intimate secrets was white lace.

The memory of that first night returned to him, elusively, as Shane began removing Lindy's hose, one silky leg, then the other. Her eyes were still closed, and he leaned over and kissed her lips again. Stay with me, he said to her under his breath. Stay.

And then the hose were off and he moved himself between her legs, putting one of her legs up on the couch as the other fell uselessly aside. He felt her inner thigh clench as he placed a wet kiss on it, and then he simply placed his whole mouth over the white lace and kissed her through it.

Lindy shuddered and turned her head to the left. The thought that resistance was futile filtered through her mind, and the fact that this phrase came from *Star Trek* flickered into her consciousness and out again just as quickly. She could think of nothing but what Shane was doing to her, and the massive release he'd already teased out of her body.

She fisted the side of the sofa in a weak attempt to get a grip on something, anything, but found herself denied as Shane's mouth pulled down the lace and tossed it somewhere aside.

She opened her eyes and saw Shane's blond head concentrated on nothing but her pleasure. He looked up at her, and his gaze locked onto hers. The intensity in his baby blues scared her, and as he brought her to rapture's edge again, she let her head fall back onto a cushion.

The thought crept into her mind, then, that she should stop him, stop *this,* but she'd ached for Shane Jacobsen for far too long. And he was making love to her because he wanted *her,* and Lindy couldn't deny herself one last pleasure, one last time.

"Take off your shirt," he said, somewhere between subsequent kisses, and powerless to resist anything, Lindy unbuttoned her blouse and let it fall to the side as another wave of pleasure overtook her.

"White lace," he murmured as he brought his face back toward hers, stopping again to kiss each breast into full extension. He stood and reached for her hand. "Come."

Maybe it was the command, maybe it was the double-edged promise in the word, but Shane had always been her pied piper, and this time was no different. She took his hand and let him lead her to her bedroom. A soft click indicated he'd closed the door behind them.

He'd seen the inside of her room, of course, but he'd never been *in* there with her. No man had. Maybe it had been the fear of the awkwardness of Tina seeing the gentlemen callers the next morning. Maybe it had just been Lindy keeping her space pure and preserved. But now as Shane pulled back her comforter and set her down on her sheets, she was glad she'd never had any memories of any other man in this bed.

His lips found hers again, and while kissing him she ran her hands up underneath his shirt. His skin felt unbelievable, incredible. She ran her fingers over his body, touching him everywhere. She tugged his shirt, and as if sensing her intentions, Shane broke their kiss, pulled it off, and tossed it aside.

Lindy closed her eyes as his lips found hers again, and she palmed him, memorizing his steel chest using nothing but her deliberate touch. In the blackness that was somehow light, she felt her bra disappear and Shane's mouth once again taste her.

"Do you know how much I want you?" he whispered, and Lindy didn't know, but as her desire for him swept over her again, she didn't care. She arched her back, and he slid his mouth down one last time before coming to rest over her on all fours. She reached for the buttons of his shorts that were now positively offensive because of the fact that they were still on.

"Look at me," he said.

She opened her eyes. His face was close to hers, those blue eyes intense. Not one part of his body touched hers, and she missed the heat that had fused between them.

Shane leaned down and gave her lips a quick kiss. "I need to know. Do you want this?"

Did she? Lindy blinked.

"I don't remember asking you last time. Now that we're both sober, this time I want you to be sure."

Maybe it was the way his eyes seemed to twinkle and the lines around his eyes crinkled that took the edge off how serious Shane's question was. Maybe it was just her overwhelming need to once again have the reality that had been her fantasy for almost three years. Maybe she just missed the warmth of his touch.

Whatever it was, right now she needed Shane Jacobsen as much as she needed to breathe. "Yes. I'm sure," she said.

And with that, he lowered himself to her, kissing her everywhere at least twice until finally he poised himself and drove himself inside her.

"Oh, my," he muttered, but Lindy had no real comprehension of Shane's dilemma, as her body had already detonated into slivers of shimmery lights. She could feel him, skin to skin.

And she'd thought her chocolate shake had been heaven. Shane joined to her was heaven. This one moment in time was nirvana, a bliss that only two people could create. A small tear formed in her right eye as the enormity of the passion Shane called from her overtook her again. He moved her as no other man ever had, probably as no other man ever would. Shane Jacobsen was her sexual other half.

She let herself go again, taking the pleasure he offered her, joining herself to his body so that the sensations that both of them experienced blended into one, as if their mutual passions had fused.

She felt him thrust deep into her and knew he was watching her face, watching her pleasure, and she kept her eyes tightly closed as Shane cried out with his own overwhelming reaction. She felt him shudder and she was with him, spiraling over the edge with him, giving and taking until both of them drifted into the sweet aftermath of spent passion.

Neither said anything, and Shane gathered her into his arms. Lindy lay across his chest, not caring that sunset seeped through the window. For right now, she was at peace, and she didn't want anything to disturb it.

A rare satisfaction overtook her, and without meaning to, Lindy slept.

SHE AWOKE to a darkened room, only to discover the smooth sensations soothing her head were Shane's fingertips stroking her hair and spreading it along the pillow. "Hey, sleepyhead," Shane said.

Lindy bolted straight up, clocking him in the chin in the process. He rolled over onto his back. "Ow."

"Sorry," she mumbled, quickly clutching the sheet to cover her naked breasts. Her own head now throbbed from the hard impact, but she ignored it. She'd just made love to Shane Jacobsen—again.

Hadn't she learned her lesson the first time? The first time had knocked her up. Lindy sighed. Where fools feared to tread, she rushed right on in, especially where Shane Jacobsen was concerned. He'd asked her if she'd wanted to stop, and she'd pressed on. But how could she have stopped? Making love to Shane was like being offered chocolate milkshakes and being asked if she wanted one. Duh. No contest there. But the end result? Now she'd another moment of delicious decadence that would live on her thighs forever.

"You have a hard head," Shane said. His words returned her from her reverie, and as Lindy's eyes adjusted to the low light, she could see a small reddish spot on his forehead.

"Sorry," she said again. "You surprised me. I mean, this surprised me. I mean…" Her voice faltered. She sounded like a babbling idiot. "How long have I been asleep?"

"Not long. About an hour and twenty-five minutes."

No way! She stared at him. "I've been asleep an hour?"

"And twenty-five minutes."

Lindy clutched the sheet a little tighter. "I—"

"You needed the rest." Shane sat up, the portion of the sheet covering him slipping down to his waist. Lindy stared at his smooth torso, the one she'd palmed with wild abandon once again. He reached forward and moved a strand of her hair out of her eyes. "You needed the rest, sweetheart."

His use of the endearment surprised her, and she turned to stare at him. "Why did you do this?"

He blinked at her, his expression clueless. "Do what?"

"Make love to me?"

"Because I wanted to," Shane said simply. Letting her right hand continue to clutch the sheet, he took her free hand in his. Warmth flowed through her. "We have a phenomenal chemistry between us. I have to admit, it's like nothing I've ever experienced. You?"

Lindy debated lying. But how could she? The passion between Shane and her was unlike any she'd ever known before. No matter what, even if it came back to haunt her, he deserved to know that. "No. I'll admit, it's pretty intense."

"Exactly. While I was kissing you I didn't want to stop. I wanted to make things right between us, to let us both feel once again what we'd done to create our baby." He reached his other hand over and placed it on Lindy's still-flat stomach. "This little one's lucky if that was the way he or she was conceived."

"We have good sex," Lindy said.

"That we do," Shane admitted. "Which is why if you won't marry me, I still want you to move in with me."

Lindy stared at him. Surely he wasn't serious. How could she live with Shane Jacobsen? She tried to lighten the moment. "Have you been watching the Disney Channel too?"

His brow furrowed as he tried to place her statement. "Disney Channel? I have no idea what you're talking about."

"Two parents live together to raise children separated at birth, it's a show. Oh, never mind. I'm sure we'll get enough of Disney Channel as junior here grows up."

"And I want to be there for that," Shane said. He kissed Lindy's cheek. "Don't shut me out, Lindy. We could be good together, and we'll be good parents. If you won't marry me, live with me. If it doesn't work out, then you can always leave. But it *will* work."

"You're forgetting one small factor."

"What?"

"Your mother and father. Can you see the headline? Prodigal son living in sin with knocked-up PA."

"I don't care what the papers say," Shane said. "I care about what you say. I want to be there, Lindy, for every moment."

"I'm not going to marry you and I'm not going to live with you, either," Lindy said.

"Why won't you marry me?"

Was it really that easy? How she wished. "You don't love me," she said. "I want to marry for love, Shane."

"So did I," he said simply. His hand, which had been on hers, now fell away. "I always thought it would be romantic. Bells. Whistles. Flowers. Something. Maybe that's why I never found it with any of the women I dated. Maybe it doesn't even exist." He shifted.

"But, Lindy, we have a baby to consider. A child who needs two parents. We get along. We don't fight, well, we didn't. We have great sex. And Lindy, I don't want to be one of those dads who hangs out at a fast-food place on the weekends. I want to be home with my child, and with my child's mother."

Lindy shifted to look at him. "Fast food?"

"Yeah, you know, pizza and playland for children. Where all the divorced parents take their kids for quality time. I found it a parental meat market."

Lindy was still trying to grasp the reference. "How do you know about those places?"

"Bethany has children, you remember my nieces and nephews? She says they're packed with people, all tolerating the noise of kids running amuck in playland, and when I was there for Bradley's birthday party I saw it for myself. Not only that, but no less than four single mothers gave me their phone numbers."

"Oh."

His eyes pleaded for understanding. "Don't make

that my fate, Lindy. If I have to go to a place like that, I want you with me. We'll tolerate the parental bliss of it all together.''

Her fingers relaxed on the sheet a little, but she didn't lower it. ''Shane, marriage isn't about fast-food places.''

He shook his head, agreeing with her. ''No, it's about partnership. We've always had that from day one, when you first came to work for me. We have a history of working well together. That tells me that we can make this,'' he gestured around, ''work.''

''But love…'' Lindy began.

''Doesn't have to factor into it. Don't you read those men-are-from-Pluto books?''

''Mars,'' Lindy corrected.

''Whatever. It's all about people and their miscommunications about love. We won't have those problems, which means that we've got a better chance of our marriage succeeding than most people do. And I won't cheat on you, Lindy. I swear it. And it will let us explore this chemistry as long as we both want.''

He reached over and ran a finger down the side of her face. Her skin prickled, and she realized that she already wanted him again.

''Don't turn me out in the cold, Lindy. Let me be the one to make love to you at night. Let me help you with baby feedings.''

She stared at him, wondering. She'd seen Shane argue in business, and he'd often persuaded her as well. But lately she'd stood up to him. She could stand up to him again, but it was hard to use your backbone when it was naked and turned to a noodle with just one of Shane's kisses.

He must have sensed her weakening. "Lindy, I want you. I want to be a family with you. Do you want some other woman to reap the benefit of three years of your influence?"

No! Jealousy flared through Lindy, and she twisted the sheet between her fists. He'd pulled out the final weapon, and Lindy suddenly knew that this was it. He'd never ask again.

But she also knew that he'd never love her. Was the sacrifice worth it? She'd hated the past two weeks without him. He'd invaded every part of her life. Was getting most of him better than having nothing?

Sensing her indecision, Shane said, "Take some time to decide. My offer of marriage still stands, but right now I'll admit, I can't concentrate on anything else but you." He leaned over and reached for her hand. Her sheet slipped. "If I may be so bold as to show you, this is what you do to me, Lindy Brinks."

And as he placed her hand on the part of him that bulged and strained, Lindy knew exactly what he was talking about. "Talk's done, and the decision can wait. But I can't. Kiss me," he murmured. He left her hand there, and threaded his free hand into her blond hair, pressing her face toward his lips.

Immediately his kiss swept Lindy away, and as the roller-coaster of his body and hers began again, Lindy knew she would ride it over and over until it finally stopped. And it would stop.

That thought crept in, worming its way through the

delightful decadence of Shane's mind-drugging kisses. Could she handle that day? The one where Shane walked out of her life?

He'd promised he wouldn't. But in her experience with relationships, promises were easily made and more easily broken. His hand had lowered to her breast, and she knew that without a doubt she wanted the chemistry to explode between them. She wanted his lovemaking, again.

She'd always wanted it.

And she knew she'd take it until the ride closed down, until Shane Jacobsen discarded her like a worn toy. Her fixation on her principles and her future faded into oblivion as he placed a line of kisses along the side of her neck.

She tried once again to focus. She knew she loved him. She knew he would never love her. Could it be enough? Would it be fair to the baby? Would it be fair to her? Could she live that way, waiting without a hope of love until the day he left her?

His lips found her breast, and thoughts of the future fled from Lindy's consciousness. Her body began to quake as the passion between them took over. She'd worry later.

Later.

Later, around five in the morning when Shane told her he had to get home. "It's a work day tomorrow. You have about two more hours of sleep."

"I'm tired," Lindy said. She rolled over and Shane began running a forefinger across her back.

"Call in sick," he teased.

That thought was so tempting. She'd slept little all night. And at the same time, his finger on her skin felt oh so good. "I can't," she managed to say. "It's only my second day."

Shane kissed her skin, and she shivered with frustrated anticipation. "I'll fix it with the boss. I think he'd agree that making love with one of his vice presidents, who happens to also be his grandson, is much more important than doing some mindless paperwork. Want me to call him? He's an early worm. He's always up by six."

Those words woke Lindy up. She jolted, and this time Shane managed to get out of the way of her upward movement. "What? You'd call your grandfather? You wouldn't dare."

Shane's grin was wicked. "Try me. You'll have to do something quick to prevent me from calling."

"Uh! You're not playing fair."

"Open lips," he mused, and he swept his down. He broke the kiss a few minutes later. "I never play fair, but in your case I'll try. If I keep kissing you, I'll never leave."

"Go," Lindy commanded.

"Going," he said. "But have lunch with me today."

Doubt plagued her. It was one thing to make love where no one knew about it. But to be public at work, even as friends? "I don't know if that's a—"

Shane lifted her fingers to his lips and kissed the ends before replying. "It's a boss's order. My office. Twelve-fifteen sharp."

"I'll have to see and…"

"Don't make me come get you," Shane teased. "Your little cubicle doesn't have a door."

This time Lindy knew he was joking. "You wouldn't."

He leaned and kissed her again. "I might. Right now I want to call both of us in sick and roll you over and bury myself deep. I want to hear you cry out my name, and claw at my back."

"Shane!" Despite herself, his talk had aroused her. She was definitely wide-awake.

"What?" He was tempting her, sucking on her fingertips again.

Lindy had always been a take-charge woman. And now with Shane in her bed she felt empowered, and insatiable. She also knew that this moment was her brass ring, and that she'd need to ride the carousel of Shane Jacobsen for as long as the ride lasted. She let the sheet drop to her waist. "So you can fix it with the boss? Make sure I don't get fired?"

"I think so," Shane said. "If not, you can always go back to work for me. Although we'd never get any work done." His mouth moved forward hungrily.

"That's good," Lindy said as the waves took over her body once again, "because I think we're both too sick to work today."

"Definitely," Shane said between kisses.

"MR. JACOBSEN, this is Alice in personnel. I thought you might like to know that your new hire Melinda

Brinks has called in sick. You do know that this is only her second day on the job.''

''Really?'' Grandpa Joe looked at the clock. Just a little past nine. As always, Alice was efficient. After thirty-five years in Jacobsen personnel, Alice still hated it when Grandpa Joe upset the order of her life by hiring or transferring people according to his business whims. Of course, he had asked Alice to personally watch over Lindy.

''Yes, Mr. Jacobsen. Miss Brinks had several personnel training sessions this morning. Normally I wouldn't call you, but you asked and…''

''You did fine, Alice. Just reschedule her appointments and be sure not to give Miss Brinks any trouble about her absence when she returns. I know her personally, and something important must have come up for her to miss today. I'm sure she's legitimately sick.''

''Yes, sir.''

Grandpa Joe put the phone down and glanced across his desk. ''Problems?'' Andrew asked. The two men always started their day with breakfast together.

''Lindy called in sick.''

Andrew's eyes narrowed with concern. ''She's never sick. Do you suspect something's wrong with the baby?''

Grandpa Joe smiled. ''No. I don't think it's anything worrisome like that. I think it's lack of sleep. It seems my grandson, our newest vice president, has also called in sick.''

"You're kidding." Andrew took a bite of blueberry muffin.

"Nope. He left me a message about six-forty this morning. The caller ID unit on my phone shows that the call came from Lindy's apartment."

"You old coot."

Grandpa Joe shook his head. "It's not for sure yet, but I'd say within a week we'll be setting a date for a quick little wedding. In fact, I'd bet on it."

Andrew laughed as he reached for his coffee. "Oh, no. I've lost too many bets to you in the past few years. I'm not even touching this one."

Grandpa Joe shrugged. "Oh, well. But you have to admit I'm right."

"I've been doing that too many times lately, too," Andrew said. "Just hope this won't backfire like it did at first with Harry and Megan."

"It won't," Grandpa Joe said. "Although at some point we're going to have to get them out of bed and back to work."

"That," Andrew said with a grin, "is your problem."

TINA WAS LONG GONE by the time Shane and Lindy left the bedroom. "Do you think she knows you were here?" Lindy asked.

"My Corvette's outside and your car is here. She's probably figured it out."

"Oh."

Shane dropped a kiss on her forehead. "Relax. We're a couple. It'll be okay." He opened her freezer.

"All you have is frozen pancakes. What about real ones? Doesn't anyone make real ones anymore?"

Lindy's thoughts were still a few paces behind. They were a couple? She blinked. "I like frozen pancakes. They're better than nothing. After all, I don't have a cook."

"I don't, either. My parents do."

"Same difference. You just call the main kitchen and get room service brought to the pool house. Ha, that'll stop when you move out. You'll find yourself eating frozen pancakes. And cleaning up after yourself."

"I hadn't thought about that," Shane said. "I guess I'll have to hire a housekeeper. Unless you can make pancakes?"

"Of course, I can. The frozen kind." Lindy drew two plastic packages from a box in the freezer. "Two minutes to yum-yum."

Shane frowned. "I'll hire us a cook, too."

She opened the packages and put the contents on two respective plates. "You're making disparaging remarks about my cooking?"

"Or lack thereof? Yes."

"A housekeeper and a cook?"

"Who else is going to cook and clean? You know I don't do it. I don't think I've ever used one of those things you call, what is it, a toilet scrubber. And do you want to do it?"

"No."

"Well, then, we'll hire someone. We can afford it. Besides, that way we won't fight over who has to do

it. We have a baby to think of.'' He took the plates
from her hands and put them on the countertop. ''I'll
make you happy, Lindy. I promise.''

She looked into his eyes. His Jacobsen blues indicated that Shane meant every word he'd just said.

And he did make her happy. Even without love.
He'd always been her best male friend. He'd been the
best lover of her life. Was settling for friendship and
passion better than holding out for a love she might
never find? If she married him, he would never leave
her. Well, at least not physically.

And there was a baby to add to the entire equation.

She just needed to remember that she could never
change him. She could never make him love her. As
long as she remembered that.

She took his hands into hers and took a deep breath.
''Shane.''

''Yes?''

The words surprisingly didn't get stuck on her
tongue. ''I will marry you.''

He gave a whoop of joy and swept his lips back
down to hers. With a swoop, he drew Lindy up into
his arms and carried her back to her bedroom, the
microwave pancakes thawing and forgotten on the
kitchen counter.

''ANYTHING ELSE?'' Andrew asked as he stopped by
Grandpa Joe's office at four o'clock. Today Henrietta
was home, meaning Grandpa Joe left the office at exactly five.

Grandpa Joe set a file folder down. ''Shane called.''

Andrew stepped inside and closed the door. "And?"

"He and Lindy are taking the next two weeks off. Something about buying a new car, finding a house and planning a wedding."

"I'm glad I didn't bet you," was all Andrew said.

Chapter Seven

"I now pronounce you husband and wife." Blake Jacobsen lowered the black leather prayer book and smiled. He closed the missal and drew it to his waist. "Shane, you may kiss your lovely bride."

Upon hearing her new father-in-law's words, Lindy blinked. So all this was actually real—the flowers, the candles, the songs, this whole beautiful ceremony. It was real. She hadn't been dreaming. Shane's father had just said the magic words that she and Shane were husband and wife. She really stood here, in Graham Chapel, as a newly married woman. Tina held Lindy's white orchids and roses, and with a slight nod of her head she motioned Lindy to move.

The second of time that had passed had been imperceptible to the gathering of family and friends, and Lindy turned and faced Shane. Seeing him, standing there so tall and beautiful in his custom tuxedo, tugged at every single one of her heartstrings. God help her, for in the past six weeks before their mid-July wedding, she'd fallen even further in love with him.

He stepped forward, leaned over and kissed her,

their first kiss as husband and wife. The touch of his lips was soft and sure as his full mouth covered hers. Immediately her heart and head both swam, and she automatically brought her left hand up to touch the side of his smooth face. People would later tell her that her brilliant diamond twinkled in the after-six sunlight that beamed through the stained-glass windows of the church.

Shane had the control to keep the kiss short, and as he drew back away from her, Lindy's eyes flew open and she remembered where she was—in a church with over seven hundred in attendance watching her kiss her husband.

Her husband. She looked at Shane for reassurance, but his baby-blue Jacobsen eyes had turned a dark and murky color, so instead Lindy glanced at Blake's eyes. His Jacobsen blues remained the normal shade. With a slight dip of Blake's chin, the organist began to play the exeunt music.

"I never introduce the couple," he'd told them several weeks ago. "Everyone came to your wedding, so they know who you are. Too many brides make a big issue about being called by their husband's name." Lindy had known what Blake meant, but being old-fashioned herself, she didn't think she'd mind being called Mrs. Shane Jacobsen. She'd dreamed of it for so long, and being confident in who she was, Lindy knew she'd always have her own identity.

And now it was time to take their first steps as husband and wife. Lindy could feel Tina behind her, shifting the massive train of the designer dress Sara had insisted on. Because Lindy was pregnant and getting married in the summer, she had wanted something simple. But since she'd come down with a small cold and her morning sickness had set in again, Lindy had instead given Sara, her army of assistants, and a wedding planner the job of organizing the big day. Lindy considered it sort of fair, anyway, especially considering the fact that Shane's parents were paying for everything.

And Lindy had no complaints. Sara had done a beautiful job. The sleeveless dress that Sara had picked out hid Lindy's first-trimester figure. The chapel at Washington University had magically been free that weekend, and so had the ballroom at the country club. Tina stepped back; Olivia, who now had the bride's bouquet, handed it to Lindy.

Shane took her arm in his, his warm hand covering hers. "Shall we?"

"Sure," Lindy said, wishing her voice sounded a little more certain. Her foot wobbled and Shane steadied her before they walked down the white-velvet runner that the florist had spread down the entire length of the long aisle.

"Not so bad now, is it?" Shane's voice was light, teasing.

Except for the wedding party and the wedding co-ordinator, no one had been in the church the night before. "Not so bad," she replied, staring at hundreds of faces she didn't know.

"Just a few more feet," Shane said. "Oh, forgot.

Smile.'' The wedding photographer's flash popped. Shane patted Lindy's arm. ''Now I think we're done.''

But instead of ushering them straight to the limousine, the wedding coordinator was gesturing them to stand by a huge floral arrangement. ''Receiving line,'' she said, and within moments she had efficiently arranged Shane's parents, the entire wedding party, and even Shane's grandparents into a neat line by which the guests could all file as they left the church.

In the next forty-five minutes Lindy decided two things: one, Shane's parents had way too many friends and associates; and two, her husband was a well-bred man. Shane met everyone with a genuine and gracious smile.

''My feet hurt,'' Lindy told him during a brief lull between guests. She tried shifting her weight, but her feet had swollen in the low pumps and her action didn't help.

''How about I rub them for you later,'' Shane said. He lifted her hand to his lips for a moment, and she could see wicked promise in his eyes. The brief kiss left her absolutely speechless, and he released her hand and turned to calmly greet another guest. ''Hello Mr. Tipton. It's a pleasure seeing you again.''

''So how are you holding up?'' Tina asked hours later, after the first dance, after the cake cutting. The two women were alone in the country club's posh ladies' lounge.

''My feet don't hurt anymore,'' Lindy said. ''That coordinator thought of everything, even custom slippers to wear after the first dance.''

"That's great. And everything else?"

"It's fine," Lindy said. Tina reached over and reattached a missing bustle hook.

Tina caught Lindy's gaze in the mirror. "I know you, Lindy. Whenever you say it's fine, it's really not. So if it's not, what else is it? You have a wonderful new house in Ladue, of all places." Tina digressed for a moment. "I still don't believe you're moving to Ladue. How many acres do you have?"

"Three," Lindy said. "Three acres on a private drive so junior can run."

Tina smoothed out a fold in the bustle. "I thought you didn't know what sex the baby is."

"I don't," Lindy said. "I'm having an ultrasound in three weeks. My doctor says I'll be able to find out then if I want, if we get a good look. So right now I just call the baby junior. It's more personal than calling it, well, it."

"So then tell me what's wrong?" Tina stepped back and gazed at Lindy without the use of the mirror. "It's not been the sex, has it?"

Lindy blushed, her pink cheeks a direct contrast to the not-quite pure-white dress being reflected in the mirror. "No, it's not the sex. That is definitely not a problem."

Far from it. Ever since she and Shane had found themselves in her bed that night at her apartment, making love to him hadn't been a problem. The problem was keeping their hands off each other, for every time he kissed her she wanted him, and vice versa.

No, they'd taken two weeks off from work to buy

a house and plan a wedding. But Sara, her staff and the wedding coordinator had quickly assumed control of everything. Once Shane and Lindy had found a house, the first day out looking, they'd spent the rest of the time, before returning to work, holed up in Shane's bed at the pool house. After all, she had had some morning sickness, and besides, the Jacobsen estate had been the best place to hide out from the press. The newspaper had been full of wedding gossip and speculation— Had Shane truly reformed? Or was he just marrying Lindy for the baby?

Lindy, though, knew the truth. He was marrying her because of the baby. He still didn't love her. Sure, they had great sex. Phenomenal, mind-altering sex. But no matter how much she loved him—and her feelings deepened on a daily basis—Lindy knew that he still didn't feel anything besides sexual longing for her. Well, that and friendship.

It was a situation Lindy wasn't quite sure how to handle. She'd married for convenience and the baby's sake. She'd settled for security and a loveless marriage, and she knew it. And, right now, at her wedding reception, she didn't want to discuss the situation with Tina, even if Tina *was* her best friend. After all, this was Lindy's wedding night—supposedly, the happiest night of her life.

"There you are!" Sara walked into the lounge. Because her mother-in-law had diverted the conversation away from the topic of Shane, for once, Lindy was glad to see her. "I was starting to get worried. Are you changing?"

Lindy smiled wryly. Okay, maybe not *that* glad to see her. "No."

Sara looked aghast. "You need to change. You don't wear the wedding dress to the hotel. That's tacky." Sara glanced around the lounge. "The suit we bought should be here somewhere. There's even shoes to match."

"Sara. Here you are." Olivia, Shane's half sister walked into the bathroom. Her baby-blue shoes matched her bridesmaid's dress, which in turn matched her and her brothers' eyes. "Sara, I'm glad I found you. Dad is looking for you. Bethany needs to leave and she wants to say a proper goodbye."

Sara's expression turned mortified. She put a finger to the brooch at her throat. "Bethany's a bridesmaid. She can't leave yet. Not until after the bride and groom."

Olivia shrugged. "Well, I think they have to get the baby-sitter home or something like that. You might want to go check it out to be sure."

Sara nodded. "Believe me, I will. Be sure you change into the suit before you come out, Lindy. I know it's in here somewhere." With that, Sara bustled out of the lounge.

Olivia turned to Lindy with a smile of amusement on her pretty face. "Are you doing okay? Shane saw his mom come in and sent me in after her." Olivia sighed. "You have to love Sara despite herself. She's an overzealous Miss Manners and Emily Post all rolled up into one. You should see her when she's on *my* case."

"Maybe Shane is wise after all," Tina said dryly.

Olivia grinned, her eyes twinkling. "Well, I do have to admit that Sara's not too bad. After all, I've known her since I was five. You learn how to manage her. You'll get used to it, Lindy. I promise." Olivia pushed a wisp of her dark brown hair off her face. "And Shane did get the best of her and Dad."

Lindy noticed that Tina didn't comment on that. "I'll be sure to tell Shane that you were sweet enough to save me," Lindy said. She'd always liked Olivia. "I'll tell him later tonight."

"Speaking of, you're not nervous about tonight are you?" Olivia suddenly blushed. "I mean, you're pregnant so your wedding night won't be the first time."

Tina peered at Olivia. "You're not saying what I think you are…you're kidding me. You're still a virgin?"

"Tina!" Lindy's tone admonished as she stared at her best friend. "That's none of our business."

Despite Lindy's reproach, Tina still looked more fascinated than repentant.

"Well," Olivia said as she blushed again. "You try having a sex in the shadow of my world-famous parents. I'm not allowed the bad boys, and just where are the good ones, anyway? They don't go out. I mean, either they're already taken or they're on-line and hiding behind a firewall. I turn thirty in two months, and besides my job and cat I have little to show for it."

"I'm divorced, so trust me, I know it's hard to find the right guy," Tina said.

"That's a gross understatement," Olivia said.

Tina nodded. "But just always remember there are worse things than being alone. Right, Lindy?"

"Right," Lindy said. She smiled. "I think."

Tina laughed. "I don't know why I asked *you*. You're married now so you don't count. As soon as you met Shane, it was all over for you."

Neither of the other two girls noticed that when Lindy smiled, it didn't quite reach her eyes. Without Shane's love, Lindy was, in essence, still alone.

"Well, I know Shane sure did some living," Olivia said. "He escaped the parents and lived enough for all of us. I wish I had half his nerve, but I'm too prim and proper to be a bad girl. Not like him. He was a wild man. Oops! Sorry, Lindy."

"Don't worry about it," Lindy said, although in truth, those years of Shane's past still needled a little, and there were memories Lindy knew she couldn't compete with. "Trust me, I worked for him for three years so I know all about him. I went into this with my eyes wide open. Believe me, when I tell you that I bought his ex-girlfriends enough trinkets to sink a ship, before sending them on their way."

"Yes, but despite that, you have to know that he's different with you," Olivia said. She paused a moment, as if searching for a convincing argument. "Seriously, Lindy. You've got to believe me when I tell you that you're special. Nick—" Olivia smiled when she mentioned her fraternal twin brother "—even commented on it. We all see a change in Shane. I mean, with you, Shane cares. He's actually interested in you because of you, not because you're the current tasty marshmallow fluff. It's good to see Shane settled.''

Olivia reached forward and gave Lindy a quick hug. ''You make him very happy, and I'm glad it's you, Lindy. I'm looking forward to really being sisters-in-law. So welcome again to the family and don't let Sara bug you too much.''

Lindy smiled. ''I'll try.''

''Good. Although, knowing Sara, you probably should get changed.'' And with that, Lindy and Tina watched Olivia leave, her baby-blue bridesmaid gown swishing around her ankles as she walked.

''She's sweet,'' Tina said.

''She is.''

Tina instantly slipped into gossip mode. ''But can you believe it? She's had no sex life.''

She was going to miss her girl talks with Tina. Even though they'd still have them, after tonight it would be different. ''It's hard to believe,'' Lindy said.

''Maybe Shane had it enough for everyone,'' Tina said. ''Oh God, sorry. It'll take me a while to get adjusted to this marriage. I'm trying to like him. Honestly, I am.''

''I know.'' Lindy sighed. For three years, Shane had always been the evil one in Tina's eyes. He'd been the reason a star-struck Lindy had never dated anyone. He'd been guilty of ignoring Lindy. In Tina's eyes, Shane was guilty of just about everything. But lately, for Lindy's sake, Tina had been trying.

''Although I reserve the right to kill him if he hurts you,'' Tina finally said.

Lindy smiled. "Hopefully it won't come to that. I'd hate for my baby to be fatherless."

"You'd control his trust fund." The look in Tina's eyes was wicked.

The two women hugged each other and broke out into laughter for a few minutes before they finally sobered. "It was a good thought," Tina teased.

"True," Lindy acknowledged. She'd held her stomach during her laughing spree, and she released her arms. She hadn't realized until this moment how much she was going to miss living with Tina. They'd been together for what seemed like forever, and as of tonight, it officially ended.

"You just let me know if you need me," Tina said. "I'll help you. Promise me."

"I promise, but I doubt it will be necessary. Actually, he didn't sow as many oats as people think. He dated a lot of women, but he didn't sleep with even a quarter of them."

"As long as you're happy with him."

Lindy took a deep breath. "I hope to be."

The two women looked at each other in the mirror. Tina placed her hand on Lindy's shoulder. "I worry about you settling," Tina said. "I worry about you—you need love, Lindy."

"I know you do," Lindy said. "But Shane's not one to really ever admit deep feelings. I've learned to live with that."

"That's not good enough, Lindy. You've been putting your heart out to Shane for three years and he hasn't noticed yet. You're a passionate woman and you deserve it all. Do not settle for no real response from him. If he doesn't respond, Lindy, you're just going to have to bring it up.''

Lindy stomped her foot in frustration, the slipper making little noise. ''I don't want to talk about it right now, Tina. Shane and I married for better or worse. I have a beautiful house, enough money that I'll never have to worry, a great job, and a baby on the way. I'm going to be happy. He just doesn't love me like I love him. That's my sacrifice. That's what I'm going to have to live with. It's not too much of a price to pay.''

Tina whirled Lindy around so they could face each other. ''Yes, it is too much of a price to pay. Believe me, marriage is hard work and I failed at it. I don't want to see you make the same mistake. You'll probably have to beat Shane on the head with a frying pan or something because he's so dense. I know that right now you're making it seem like there is no real big deal about his not loving you, but honey, we've been friends for too long. You know it does affect you. So, don't let any opportunity pass you by. It might just make things a little different for you. Who knows. I only want you to be happy, and if it's Shane Jacobsen, then well, he at least better love you.''

''I'm not holding out any hope. Can we please drop this?''

Tina squeezed Lindy's hands. ''Okay. We'll talk later. You're right, tonight's not the time. How about we get you out of that dress and into your suit before your mother-in-law comes in here breathing fire again. It's in here somewhere, right?''

''Supposedly. And my changing is probably a good idea,'' Lindy acknowledged. ''Sara mentioned something about how it's bad form to leave before the bride and groom, and there are people who probably want to leave.''

About five minutes later, Lindy stared at herself in the mirror. She now wore a not-quite-white designer suit that flattered every inch of her figure.

''You still look beautiful,'' Tina said. ''I love you dearly, you know.''

''I know, and I couldn't have done any of this without you. Thanks for being my best friend.'' Lindy smiled wistfully. ''Do you mind? Can you give me a few minutes?''

Tina nodded. ''Sure. I'll go tell Sara that you're dressed and will be out in a moment.''

''That'll be great.'' Lindy stared at herself in the mirror as Tina left the lounge. She had to admit it to her reflection; she did look pretty. No wonder celebrities always look great, Lindy thought. If I had their entourage, I could look this good every day too. She placed a hand protectively over her abdomen. It was too soon to feel any movements.

''Oh, sorry. I thought it was empty.''

Lindy turned as Wendy Grisman-Hawksley entered the women's lounge. Lindy had never liked the overbearing, all-knowing and ''social drinker'' Wendy much. In fact, Lindy wouldn't have even invited Wendy to the wedding, but the guest list had been Sara's doing, not Lindy's. Wendy Grisman-Hawksley had grown up next door to the Jacobsens' estate, and stayed with her parents quite frequently when her husband acted up. But her parents donated small fortunes to the ministry, and that made her a valued guest.

"The stalls are free," Lindy offered. "And I'm leaving. I had to change."

Wendy blinked as if the light was too bright. She shook her glass and the ice rattled. "Oh, yes. My mother told me about it. A night at the Ritz and then two weeks in Alaska. How quaint. Tell me, do you really think you'll be happy with him?"

Wendy had been enjoying too much of the open bar, Lindy decided. "Actually, I do."

Wendy squinted at Lindy. She covered her mouth with her hand for a moment. "You're actually serious. Oh, my poor deluded girl. You know he only married you because of the baby."

"Of course I do," Lindy replied. "But we're very happy."

"Oh, please," Wendy said. She exhaled to make her point. "He'll never love anyone at all." Wendy tottered toward the door that divided the lounge's stall area from the seating area. "At least tell me he's not still fixated on that girl from camp. His great ultimate love. What an idiot."

"How do you—" Lindy began, but she quickly stopped herself. She did not need to share Shane's secrets.

Wendy paused from putting her hand on the pull bar. "What? Were you saying something? About the girl?"

Lindy took a breath. Then again, why not probe just

a little? Knowing Wendy, she probably wouldn't remember any of the conversation in the morning. "I just wondered how you knew about her?"

Wendy held the handle for support. "I had the worst crush on Shane. I was going into seventh grade and at the end of the summer I snuck over. All he talked about was her." Wendy pushed the door open, suddenly a bit more coherent. "And he dated a few of my friends over the years. Honey, it was a great wedding, but don't get disillusioned. Hell, then you'll end up like me. He's a heartbreaker, that one."

And with that, she pushed her way through the doorway.

"Lindy?" Tina poked her head through the outer door. "Are you coming? It's time to go."

"Coming," Lindy said. She gave one last glance at her wedding dress. The wedding coordinator would be in to package the dress up and send it off for preservation.

Preserved for what, Lindy didn't know. Her daughters? A museum? She shook her head to clear her thoughts. She had no illusions when it came to Shane Jacobsen. So what if Shane didn't love her? She loved him, and that would have to be enough.

Life was all about sacrifices. She'd made those all her life. She could make them for the rest of her time on earth, too. The minute he kissed her, every bit of negative reality always fled her head. Just kissing Shane…already a heat began to travel through her. Passion. She'd cling to that. Time for the honeymoon.

Chapter Eight

Alaska was beautiful—that is, what she and Shane saw of it when they finally left their cruise ship cabin, and later their hotel room overlooking Mt. McKinley. But August soon arrived, and with the two passionate, glorious weeks over, Lindy and Shane found themselves back in St. Louis, in their new home, on the job.

Lindy had never lived with a man before. Were they all that moody? Lindy sighed as she drove her Grand Prix downtown. Normally she rode with Shane in his new sensible family sedan; it had been over a week since she'd driven herself to work. But Shane had an early-morning breakfast meeting, and today she had a doctor's appointment, so she gripped her leather-wrapped steering wheel and sang along with the radio.

In a sense, it was nice that she had the car to herself. While she and Shane listened to the same type of music, the other day he'd told her that a song by the 1980s band Tears for Fears reminded him of that girl from camp.

"She has two songs?" Lindy had asked.

"No," Shane had said as he'd pulled into the park-

ing garage. "The Tears For Fears one played during
the time we were at a dance at camp. The other song,
a Goo Goo Dolls tune, was years later when I remembered the moment."

And what's our song? But Lindy hadn't asked that
question because she already knew the answer. She
and Shane didn't have one. They really didn't have
anything in common except a baby on the way.

She entered the Jacobsen Enterprises parking garage
and pulled into her assigned space. Within moments,
she placed her purse down on her desk, in her large
new office, complete with a view, right down the hall
from Harry's wife, Megan. Amazing the perks of her
job now that Lindy bore the surname Jacobsen.

"Hey!" Megan poked her head in. "How are you
feeling?"

"Good," Lindy said. "You?"

"Great." Megan patted her tummy. "Kicking
away. Just wait your turn. You'll love the first time,
and then you can't sleep because all it does is move.
Your ultrasound is today, right?"

"Yes."

"Good luck. I'm in meetings all day, so be sure to
bring me a picture tomorrow."

"Okay," Lindy said.

"Is Shane going?"

Was he? He'd indicated yesterday that he was going
to the appointment, but he hadn't said anything about
it this morning. Then again, she'd only seen him for
five quick moments, enough for a brief kiss before
he'd slipped out the bedroom door. "I think so."

Megan grinned. "You better call his secretary and remind her. I think he's got meetings all day, but nothing that can't be rescheduled." Megan rolled her eyes. "Men. Without their secretaries they'd be nothing."

And with those parting words, Megan disappeared down the hall.

Lindy sat down and leaned back in her executive leather office chair, a far cry from the rolling cloth one she'd had in her cubicle. Megan's words resonated in Lindy's head. Men were helpless without their secretaries. She drummed her fingers against the armrest. She'd once been that secretary, that PA.

How many calls had she fielded from Shane's girlfriends? How many dates had she arranged? How many flowers, how many goodbye gifts had she sent? Lindy drew her chin up. He'd married her for the baby. They were two roommates who had great sex but, aside from that, had nothing in common except for the fact that she used to work for him.

Tina would say Lindy was moping.

Perhaps she was, but she was not going to call Shane's secretary and remind her of Shane's commitments to his wife. She would not be like those pathetic girlfriends who had called him, and then probably spent the afternoon wondering when Shane would call back or if he'd remember them at all.

Perhaps the bloom was off the rose. But she shouldn't have to call. She was his wife. She picked up a file folder and got to work.

"AND THIS IS a leg," the ultrasound technician said. The woman froze the black-and-white image on the monitor screen, and on a keyboard she typed the word *leg*. The word then appeared on the screen.

Lindy stared in fascination at the small monitor. That image on the screen was her baby. She could see his heart beating, and at one point the technician had gotten a clear picture of the baby's face. The ghostly image had looked like a little alien on the ultrasound monitor, even showing the baby's eyes, nose and mouth.

"They all look like that," the technician had said as she froze the image and typed the word *face*. "Trust me, they come out just fine."

Lindy hadn't cared about the way the ultrasound picture showed a somewhat distorted face. She simply watched in amazement as additional images appeared on the screen. The technician squeezed some more warm gel onto Lindy's stomach. "I've got to measure the head if he'll give me a good look."

They'd been referring to the baby as a boy, but Lindy still hadn't had actual confirmation. "Is it a he?"

The technician ran the wand over Lindy's stomach and captured a view of the circumference of the baby's head. "Oh, I don't know the sex yet. Do you want to know?"

"Yes," Lindy said. She craned her head a little more. "I do."

The technician gave her a quick smile. "Then if I get a good look I'll tell you. I'm going to try and get the baby's length now."

Lindy raised her head a little. "And everything looks fine?"

The technician didn't turn her gaze from the monitor. "So far, yes."

Lindy relaxed back into the pillow. The wand tickled but didn't hurt at all as the technician ran it firmly over her stomach.

A knock sounded at the door and the technician froze another image. One of the front desk workers stuck her head in. "Mrs. Jacobsen?"

It took Lindy a second to remember that she was Mrs. Jacobsen. "Yes?"

"Your husband is here. Would you like him to come in?"

Shane had made it? Lindy glanced at the clock. Three-ten. Her appointment had started at two-forty-five. "Yes. Please send him in," Lindy said. The technician had started moving the wand again, but Lindy instead watched the entrance. Within seconds, Shane strode through and shut the door behind him.

Even the low lights of the room didn't hide how handsome he was. He had shed the suit coat, unbuttoned the first two buttons on his shirt and rolled up his sleeves. He came over and dropped a quick kiss on her lips. "Sorry I'm late."

"Megan said you had meetings."

"Which I walked out of as soon as I could," Shane said. He sat on a chair and rolled himself next to the table Lindy was lying on. As he grabbed her hand, an immediate comforting warmth flowed through her. "I told you I would be here for every moment. I'm just sorry I wasn't here at the beginning. I had a video-conference that didn't start on time. So what did I miss?''

"Our baby," Lindy told him, but Shane's gaze had already located the monitor.

"That's the heart beating," the technician said with a point of her finger. "And your child is right now giving us the perfect shot that he's a boy. See?''

Both Shane and Lindy followed the technician's finger. The screen froze, and the technician started typing. The words *sex* and *boy* appeared on the screen.

"We created a boy," Shane said. "A boy." He leaned over and gave Lindy another kiss. "Thank you."

The technician pulled some black-and-white pictures out of the machine and handed a set to Lindy. "Those are yours. The rest go to your doctor. You're seeing him within the next two weeks, right?''

"Yes."

"Then we're all done here. You're free to get dressed and leave." The technician smiled and left the room.

The door had barely clicked shut behind her when Shane said, "Show me the pictures." Lindy took a minute to show him. "Our boy. I guess we do have junior after all, don't we?''

A rare happiness and contentment completely filled Lindy. "We do. A boy." As she sat up, a thought struck her. She turned to Shane. "It's a boy. I have no idea how to raise a boy."

Shane grinned, a goofy smile that covered his entire

face. "Neither do I," he said. "So we'll do it together. There's got to be an idiot's guide to raising a boy out there. I'm sure we'll manage just fine. I mean, my parents did it." He suddenly looked sheepish. "That probably doesn't inspire you with tons of confidence, does it?"

She loved it when he was sweet. "I'm sure we'll do fine." Lindy swung around to get off the table. "I'm going to get dressed."

Shane's finger snaked forward and he twirled a strand of her hair around his finger. "I like you undressed," Shane said.

"Down, boy." Lindy teased. She slid away from him, and totally unembarrassed by her bra and panty-clad body in his presence, she pulled off the gown.

"Yeah, right. Look at you dressed like that. I know this isn't the time or place, so I'll give you fair warning. I'll wait only until we get home."

The low lights danced in his now-darkened eyes. "I want to be inside you, Lindy. I want to feel you, to believe we created something so magical." He put his arms around her. "Hey. Sticky."

She drew away with a grin. "That'll teach you for being greedy." She reached for some towels the technician had left, and began to clean her stomach. "It's the gel for the ultrasound. Now why don't you scoot on home and I'll meet you there."

"I'll wait." To give her privacy, Shane turned his back and pulled out his cell phone. As Lindy cleaned up and pulled on her short-sleeve sweater, she heard him bang it against his palm.

"Phone's dead," he said. "The battery hasn't been charging right for a while. I need a new one."

"Mine's in my purse," Lindy said.

She pulled on her skirt as he rummaged for it.

"Hey, Grandpa Joe," Shane said. He paused as he listened. Then Lindy heard her husband chuckle before saying, "So what if you're in a meeting and I called your private line. I did something right for once. It's a boy. A Jacobsen boy."

Lindy stopped pulling on her shoes. Shane's face was fully animated. "Yes, you heard me. A boy. What? Don't even think about it. Lindy and I can do that part ourselves. When are we coming back?" Shane laughed. "If you're lucky you'll see us in the morning."

He hit the phone's end button and smiled at Lindy. "He told us he'd help us name the baby."

"Not on his life," Lindy said.

"That's why I told him not to even think about it. Come on, Lindy, let's go home. I'm hungry."

"I am too," she admitted. "I missed lunch and…"

"Food. I wasn't referring to—" Shane groaned his frustration. "You want food. Real food."

"Oh, I knew what you meant," Lindy said with a slight cock of her head. She gave him a knowing smile. "But I want food first. I'm pregnant. You know the pregnant woman's priority chain."

"I do. And luckily for me, I know of a Steak 'n Shake drive-thru on the way home," Shane said. He drew her into his arms and gave her another kiss, this one promising the passion soon to come. "Because I have to tell you, I can't wait."

LATER THAT NIGHT, Lindy quietly slipped out of bed and headed to the ensuite bathroom. One of the more annoying changes in her body, she reflected, was the pressure on her bladder as the baby grew. Lindy found herself living in the bathroom 24/7.

She finished her business and washed her hands. She glanced at herself in the mirror. Everything about her had changed.

But one thing hadn't. Shane didn't love her.

As usual, the day's lovemaking had been wonderful, perhaps even more intense than usual. Shane had held her close, told her how much he appreciated her carrying his baby, and told her how beautiful junior was.

But he hadn't told her that he loved her, and she knew he never would.

She smiled wanly at her pale reflection and began to wash her face. She'd vowed not to try to change him. But she couldn't keep what she felt bottled up inside of her any longer. She had to tell him how she felt. She had to let the chips fall where they may. Tina had said about the same thing that night of the wedding reception.

Lindy shook her head. Tina was wrong. Telling Shane would be wrong. It would put him in that awkward position of having a woman love him, a woman that he couldn't, and never would, love. After all, Shane didn't even believe in love, well, not counting that girl at camp fourteen years ago.

As for Lindy's feelings…she turned the water off. She had to be honest with herself. She was pregnant. She craved Ho Ho's and Steak 'n Shake. Her feelings? They were all hormones. Feeling not a bit better for her rationalization, she dried her hands and walked back into the bedroom.

The massive house still amazed her. Although located in an older neighborhood, their house on Upper Ladue Lane was actually brand-new. Lindy had seen the real estate sheet—the land had been $750,000, and then the existing house on the property had been torn down. Lindy had four thousand square feet of new house, and Shane hadn't blinked at signing the paperwork on their multimillion-dollar purchase.

Even though she worked for him, and was well aware of Shane's social stature, Lindy hadn't ever really thought about his wealth. When she was on her own, she'd always had enough money to get by. But now as Shane's wife, she was rich. His wealth made her every desire possible, all but one.

She'd sold her soul and settled for a house, security and a life without love. And there was nothing she could do about it. Frankly, it terrified her.

"Hey," Shane said. She could make out his silhouette when she returned to the bed. He was sitting up. "Everything okay?"

"Baby on my bladder," she said.

"I missed you the moment you were gone." He lifted the sheet for her. "I guess I'll have to get used to these late-night trips."

"Probably," Lindy replied. She glanced at the clock

before she slipped back under the sheet. The bright red display read 1:00 a.m. Odd. She'd thought it was much later.

He leaned over to kiss her. As his lips touched hers, Lindy melted. Would it always be this way? Would he always have the power to turn her into putty, and then raise her to peaks she didn't know existed?

Would she always love him?

Probably. And as she always did, she told him her feelings the only way she felt safe—with her body.

"Good night, darling," Shane said as he pulled her into his arms later.

Lindy snuggled in deeper next to him, her body spent. She couldn't have moved her legs or her arms even if she'd wanted to. As always, their lovemaking had been nothing short of incredible.

She smiled slightly as the sandman crept in. The solution to her problem suddenly seemed so simple. She didn't need to say the words "I love you" aloud. She'd just say them quietly to herself each time they made love. That way Shane could never reject her.

She'd never…have to say…"I love you."

But in the haze of oncoming sleep, the words escaped her before she could call them back. She heard Shane whisper "shh," then wondered if she'd really said anything at all.

Shane held his breath, waiting as he always did until Lindy fell asleep first. He liked watching her in the dark; he liked listening to her breathe, a steady inhale and exhale of perfect peace.

But not tonight. Tonight, trouble had crept into his orderly world.

Tonight Lindy had said those three scary little words.

Sure, other women had told him they'd loved him, but he'd never believed them, never really even cared.

Love didn't actually exist, and after all, those women were after his fortune, his body, his social stature as a Jacobsen, or some other thing from him. But not Lindy.

No, Lindy had never wanted anything from him. In all her years of working for him, she'd never wanted more. She'd never made demands. She'd even turned down his marriage proposal. So Grandpa Joe had said to woo her, and Shane had. He'd followed all the rules. The bonus to the arrangement was the wonderful passion he and Lindy shared.

He'd married her, Lindy Brinks.

Lindy who already had it all and didn't care about the rest.

Which meant that Lindy loved him for him.

But he was a man who didn't believe in love. Despite all their mutual passion, he didn't love her.

He was male enough to recognize the kiss of death.

And it had just been dealt.

Dear God, just what was he going to do?

Chapter Nine

Shane began his day by acting as normal as possible. He got up, took a shower, shaved, and went downstairs for pancakes that Marni, the housekeeper, had prepared. He picked up the day's *St. Louis Post-Dispatch* and perused the front page. He glanced at his Rolex. He knew Lindy was up and would come downstairs shortly. As he did most mornings, he'd drive her to the office.

All should be normal. But he knew it wasn't. He'd heard words that, once said, could never be retracted. Even though Lindy had been almost asleep when she'd mumbled her declaration of love, Shane had heard it. It was now "out there."

Somewhere in the middle of the commentary page, Shane thought that maybe, if he pretended Lindy hadn't said "I love you," then she wouldn't remember saying it at all. She had been nearly asleep, and probably thought she was already in some dream.

But he knew that wouldn't work. Pretending he hadn't heard what she'd said would be just about as bad as Lindy's concealing from him that he'd slept with her after his birthday party. They didn't need lies between them and not telling her was akin to lying.

At some point, he was going to have to tell her what he'd heard.

It just didn't have to be right at this second, Shane thought, as Lindy entered the kitchen. As always, to him, she was beautiful. Her dark blond hair was tucked into a bun that, already, his fingers itched to tear apart. She wore a simple sundress with a matching cardigan sweater, and now that it was August, she skipped the panty hose, opting for bare legs and sandals. Despite being casual, she still looked totally professional.

"Hi," she said as she sat down at the table. "Sleep well?"

"Great," Shane fibbed. "You?"

"I think I tossed and turned a little bit, but other than that I don't remember a thing. No dreams. Nothing."

"Nothing?"

She frowned. "No. Should I? Did I elbow you or something?"

"No, you kept to your side," Shane said. He grinned at her. Lindy usually tried to hog the whole bed.

"Good." The housekeeper set a grapefruit in front of Lindy. She stared at it.

Shane knew instantly that something was wrong. "Don't you like grapefruit? You used to eat it."

"I love it. But right now I feel as if…" Lindy pushed the grapefruit away. "I hate these hormonal changes. Megan told me she used to love turkey. Now the sight of a turkey club makes her ill. She's eating roast beef instead.''

Marni came back over. ''Miss?''

''I'm sorry, Marni. For some reason the thought of taking a bite of this turns my stomach. Would you mind bringing me some Cocoa Puffs?''

Marni shook her head, but didn't contradict or ask questions. ''I take it that baby likes sugary chocolate cereal. Well, I will get him some. Milk, too?''

''Please.''

Shane watched Marni disappear into the kitchen. Since his grandmother Henrietta had refused to part with Cindy, the family cook and Shane's first nanny, Cindy had recommended Marni. So far she'd been an absolute gem. It had taken Lindy a little while to get adjusted to having live-in help, but as with most things, Lindy was doing fine.

Shane had to give his wife credit. He wasn't the easiest man to live with, but so far Lindy had been able to sense when he needed space, and let him retreat into his home office without fussing over him like an insecure mother hen. There were times when he needed her, and she had been right there; other times, she'd simply read a book while he relaxed by playing a video game.

And unlike several former girlfriends, Lindy trusted him to check his personal e-mail without wanting to look over his shoulder and know who sent what.

Maybe it was the house. There was plenty of room for two people. For two people and a baby, there would still be room to spare.

They'd already picked out the room that would serve as the nursery. Lindy had said it was still too soon to decorate, so right now the room sat totally empty of furniture, still painted contractor-white.

Much to his surprise, Shane had actually found himself interested in what the nursery would look like. Lindy hadn't even started looking at wallpapers or contacting decorators. ''I'll nest later,'' she'd told him. ''I'm not due until January. That's five months from now.'' He hadn't protested.

''So what's on your agenda today?'' Lindy's voice brought Shane back to the moment.

''Meetings,'' he told her. ''Grandpa Joe is thinking about expanding again. There's been some interest in bringing some Jacobsen's Restaurants to a few more locations in the Northeast. I'm in charge of the preliminary site review. We're hearing the results of the scouting reports today.''

''I should probably drive myself to work,'' Lindy said.

Shane frowned slightly. Was she avoiding him? ''That's really not necessary. I'll be done by lunch. It should be a normal day after that. I can take you.''

''I thought I might make some stops on the way home,'' Lindy replied. ''Your mother gave me the name of an interior designer and told me I had to stop by her shop. You know how your mother is, especially when she's trying to wrap up what she considers to be loose ends.''

Shane grimaced. Although he'd just been thinking about the nursery, his mother's involvement in something often spelled annoying times ahead. "She's worried about the nursery now, isn't she?"

Lindy nodded as she finished her bite of cereal. "She's afraid that if I don't get on the designer's schedule now, I won't make it at all. I mean, really. It's not like the baby will notice. I want to put a bassinet in our room for the first six weeks anyway."

"Mom means well, but she can be a little overzealous."

Lindy toyed with her spoon. "I guess she has to be, with the frantic pace of your father's ministry. There's also the little fact that the designer's services are your parents' present to us."

Shane folded the paper. "Well, let's look on the bright side. Luckily for us, they'll be leaving in two days for a stadium tour in California. They'll be gone through Labor Day."

"What's it called again, the Labor of Love tour?"

"Yeah. They're hitting Los Angeles, San Francisco and San Diego. Three nights in each city. They plan to be back for Nick and Olivia's thirtieth birthday party. That's September 15."

"It's already marked on my calendar," Lindy said. "Family only, in Henrietta's private room." Lindy mentioned the location of the event, at Jacobsen Enterprise's five-diamond, five-star signature eatery.

"At least they won't miss that," Shane said.

"Shane." Lindy's tone sent a mild reprimand.

He rolled his eyes. "I know. Sorry. But it still rankles that they forgot my twenty-fifth. Although, I guess something good came out of it. We're having our son.'' And for that he would be forever grateful to Lindy.

He glanced at his watch again, got up and dropped his napkin on the table. He walked around the table and put his hands on Lindy's shoulders. Her skin felt magical beneath his touch. He stroked her neck. Oh, if he didn't have meetings... ''Take care today, darling, and I'll see you tonight.''

She looked up at him, the sunlight reflecting on her brown eyes. ''I'll have Marni plan dinner for right around six-thirty.''

''That sounds perfect,'' Shane said. His next words caught in his throat, and without saying anything, he left the dining room, leaving Lindy alone.

''Chicken.'' He chastised himself aloud as he walked toward the four-car garage. He should have told her what he'd heard her say last night. Angry at himself, he ignored the sensible sedan. Today the Corvette called him. Seconds later, he turned the volume of the Pete Yorn song up to full blast and hit the highway.

SHANE HAD BEEN bothered about something. Lindy knew it. But then, Shane always had had his moods. When she'd worked for him, she hadn't been privy to so many. Now that she was married to him and with him 24/7...Lindy sighed as she watched the Corvette speed down the long driveway and out of view. He loved that car.

Funny how a man could love a car, but not a woman.

She shook her head to clear that negative thought and finished the last few bites of her cereal. As always, the Cocoa Puffs had turned the white milk chocolatey. She stood and reached for her bowl, but Marni was too quick for her. All her life Lindy had washed her own dishes; now she didn't even have to carry them to the kitchen. "Marni, is dinner at six-thirty okay?"

Marni smiled. "Just fine, miss. I'm going to barbecue steak and chicken. Cindy told me how much Shane likes that, and it's supposed to be a great night for dinner on the terrace."

"That sounds perfect. Thank you." Lindy watched Marni leave. Never in a million years would Lindy have ever thought about being a housekeeper, but it amazed her how much money live-in help actually commanded. Marni was wonderful, and would be a perfect nanny for the baby, when he arrived. Freed from dishes and other chores, Lindy had nothing else to do but go to work.

For the first time, for some strange reason, she really didn't want to go to work. She reached for her cell phone and dialed Tina.

"Hey," she said when Tina finally answered.

"Hey," Tina's groggy voice said. "This better be good, Lindy."

Lindy smiled. Tina wasn't human until she'd downed two cups of coffee. "Sorry to wake you, sleepyhead, but are you flying today or can you meet me for lunch?"

"I just got in four hours ago," Tina said. "I want to sleep."

"Great. We'll do lunch at one. I'll call you at eleven-thirty to make sure you're up and tell you where."

"Okay," Tina said. "One."

Lindy hung up the phone. Tina would have the answer. She always did.

"SHANE."

Upon hearing his name, Shane turned to face his grandfather. They were both standing in the boardroom, the meeting to review the restaurant scouting reports finally over at a little after one in the afternoon. "Yes?"

Grandpa Joe came over and shook Shane's hand. "Good job today."

"Thanks." The praise coming from Grandpa Joe felt, well, in Shane's opinion, pretty good. For the first time in his life, he was actually doing the right thing. Even better, now that he was active in Jacobsen Enterprises, he wondered why he hadn't done it earlier.

The job he did was invigorating, the work interesting. Grandpa Joe had found Shane an area that he thrived in, and Shane loved to use his intellect to conquer the business problems he faced. He felt like he was making a difference. What's more, he still had time to manage both his investment accounts and the Shane Jacobsen charitable foundation.

Grandpa Joe dropped Shane's hand. "Listen, I know the meeting ran a bit over. Anyway, I'm going to have some lunch sent up to my office. I'd like it very much if you'd join me."

Shane thought for a quick second. Grandpa Joe had never invited him just for lunch. Despite the fact that there might be a catch, Shane said, ''Sure.''

''Good. Do you have any preferences?''

Shane picked up his briefcase. The leather felt good and solid against his palm. ''Do they still have that salmon sandwich?''

''I'll ask,'' Grandpa Joe said. ''If not, what do you want?''

''A burger will be just fine. I have the feeling Marni is going to barbecue tonight.''

Grandpa Joe nodded. ''Very well. Shall we meet in, say fifteen minutes?''

''I'll be there.'' Shane hummed as he left the boardroom. Praise and a lunch invitation. Perhaps the prodigal son had finally been welcomed home.

Of course, he had done some reforming. Shane pressed the elevator button. He could worry about Lindy's love declaration later. At that moment he felt pretty damned good. He had to tell Lindy. She'd want to know. He pressed the button again. Just where was that elevator? Deciding not to wait another moment, Shane went down the stairs to the next level.

But when he went by Lindy's office, she wasn't there. A sharp pang of disappointment filled Shane. He headed back toward the stairwell, passing Megan's office on the way.

''Hey. Shane.''

Shane paused in Megan's doorway. She sat behind her desk, a pile of papers and three colored highlighters in front of her. "Hey, Megan, have you seen Lindy?"

Megan shook her head as she picked up the pink highlighter and underlined key words in a report. "I haven't seen her since this morning when she passed all this stuff off on me. But she did mention that she had plans for lunch with, oh, what's her name? The maid of honor from her wedding."

A small prickle ran up Shane's spine as he leaned on Megan's doorframe. Lindy at lunch with Tina was a big uh-oh, and he knew exactly what they'd be discussing. Him. "The maid of honor's name is Tina."

Megan nodded. "Right. That's it. Tina." Highlighter still in hand, Megan glanced at her watch. "Lindy's probably still at lunch. Do you need her? You could always call her on her cell phone."

"Nah." Shane shook his head and straightened up. "I only had a moment before my lunch with Grandpa Joe. I just thought I'd drop in, see how she's doing. You know our ultrasound was yesterday. It's a boy."

"I know. Lindy showed me the pictures. Congratulations."

"Thanks. Don't worry about giving her a message. I'll just catch up with her later."

Megan smiled, one of those sage, women-know-all smiles. "Oh, think nothing of it. Harry drops in all the time with one excuse or the other."

Yes, but he wasn't Harry. All anyone had to do was look at Harry to see how much he loved his wife. As for Shane, that didn't apply. He didn't love Lindy. Right?

But there was the fact that she loved him, and he knew he was going to have to deal with that sooner or later. Shane made his way back upstairs to Grandpa Joe's office.

By 1:15 p.m.—despite delicious food and several tall glasses of lemonade—Tina still didn't have any answers at all for Lindy.

Tina set her fork aside and pushed her salad away. "So you're not sure if he heard you?"

Lindy took another bite of her chocolate cake. She'd finished her roast beef sandwich ages ago, and had opted for dessert. "I'm not sure I even said it. I probably did, though, and I'm sure he heard it."

Tina reached for her lemonade. "So what's the problem with that? Like I told you before, you might need to hit him upside the head with how you feel about him. It might do him some good."

The chocolate cake suddenly tasted papery. Lindy waved her fork in the air, sending cake crumbs flying. "Or it might make him feel trapped. Pressured. Shane trapped is not an oxymoron. Those two words don't go together like *jumbo shrimp.* He'll walk away, or…"

Tina looked at Lindy over the rim of her lemonade glass. "Or what?"

Lindy put her fork down and pushed away the plate of half-eaten chocolate cake. "I'm not sure. All I know is, whatever he does, it won't be positive. That's why I've decided not to talk about it. I'll just pretend it never happened. I mean, my declaration of love did occur after sex. You and I both know that's a woman's most vulnerable time. Heck, men know that too. Isn't it their rule that nothing said in the afterglow can be held against them?''

Tina twirled her straw between her fingers. ''I don't think I'm familiar with that rule. I think if you say it, especially then, usually you mean it.''

''No. It's the height of emotion, that's all. And I'm sure it's a rule. I think it's the only one men get. I mean, you know if a guy says he loves you after casual sex he might just be being nice. You shouldn't go pick out china.'' Tina set her straw down. ''Since women get all the other rules, including the right to change their minds, I say, if it happens in the afterglow, it doesn't count,'' Lindy said.

Tina frowned. ''Lindy, I still don't necessarily like Shane. I still think he's a rat who's not good enough for you. But it doesn't matter how I feel, it's how you feel that's important. It's already out there. You must tell him the truth. Put the ball in his court. If he doesn't return it, well, then perhaps you'll have to decide what to do. Maybe he'll surprise you. I doubt it, but for your sake I'm ever hopeful. Lindy, take it from me. For your own sanity, you need to tell him how you feel.''

Lindy's lips puckered and her brow furrowed. ''I need to get away from him.''

Tina shook her head. ''That's no longer an option.''

Lindy stirred her lemonade with her straw. ''Sometimes I wish it was.''

''That's because you haven't put all your cards on

the table. You're folding before you know the score. So play the hand you dealt yourself. See where it goes. Maybe you'll win all the chips.''

Lindy rolled her eyes. "I can tell you've been flying the Las Vegas route again."

Tina grinned. "Can't you? I've got another two weeks to go and then I'm back on Chicago routes for a month."

The humorous moment passed. "Chicago's probably safer for me. With my luck, despite your advice on how to play the games, I'd probably lose all my chips."

"That's the risk you take." Tina glanced at her watch. "I wish I could stay longer, but we're going to need to get going."

Lindy signaled for the waiter. "I know. It's just been so—"

Tina interrupted Lindy by reaching over and covering her hand. "You don't have to say it. I miss you, too. I didn't realize until you moved out how much I'd come to depend on you being there. There's so much I want to say, to tell you, and you aren't around."

Lindy sighed. "I feel the same way, but I'm only a phone call away. We'll do more of these lunches. Dinner maybe. Shane doesn't control all my time."

"Ha. I know you. One kiss and it's over. Speaking of, I haven't told you that I met a new guy. I'm not sure it'll work out, but it does look promising. In fact, I'm going to meet Tom now, which is why I can't be late. He took the afternoon off so that we can go see an early movie before I have to fly out tonight.''

"So tell me about him," Lindy said, and in the ten minutes before she and Tina parted company, Lindy listened to her friend talk about her new love interest. Then it was back to the office. As Lindy stepped out of the elevator, she bumped into Megan.

"Hey," Megan said. She placed her hand on the elevator door so it wouldn't close. "Did Shane find you?"

Shane was looking for her? "No."

"Oh." Megan frowned for a quick second. "Well, he was just here, maybe about ten to fifteen minutes ago. He said he had a short break and dropped by to talk to you."

Megan stepped inside the elevator and pressed the door's open button. "He actually seemed a little embarrassed by it, but I told him Harry did it all the time. Anyway, if you need him, I think he said he's having lunch with Grandpa Joe." Megan pressed the lobby button. "I'm off to my latest doctor's appointment. I'll see you tomorrow."

"Bye," Lindy said as the polished brass elevator doors closed. She walked toward her office, stopping to ask her secretary if she'd seen Shane. She hadn't.

Lindy dropped her purse into her desk drawer and checked her voice mail. She didn't have any messages, and when she called Shane, she got his voice mail.

Wondering what he wanted, she decided to take a quick minute and hop up one floor to find out.

"SHANE, COME IN," Grandpa Joe said with a wave of his hand. "Leave the door open so that we'll know when the food gets here. My secretary's gone for the rest of the day, and no matter how I try and tell them otherwise, no one from the kitchen wants to knock on a closed door."

"So you're still intimidating the kitchen staff?"

"Ah, it's more about respect. Johnny the chef is old-fashioned. I think he's almost seventy and he's very old-school. Closed doors mean no admittance unless a secretary announces you. Ah, he's a great chef and I'll hate it when he finally retires. Luckily for me, so far he hasn't shown any inclination."

Grandpa Joe gestured toward a sofa. "So, sit. Sit. Tell me, how's everything going? Do you have one of those ultrasound pictures with you? You do know you need to stop by the house and show them to your grandmother. She's been on my case again, you know."

Shane sat on the leather couch and stared at his grandfather. He reached into his wallet and pulled out the picture that Lindy had cut out for him. "That's the baby's head," he said with a point. "And there's an arm."

"I can't tell the sex," Grandpa Joe said.

"Lindy has that picture," Shane said. "And if I can be so bold, being your grandson, you're a bit lively today."

"Probably more than usual," Grandpa Joe said as he sat across from Shane. "Not only are you having a boy, but I'm still a bit pumped from our meetings today. I love success, and this venture looks to be one of our best yet. I guess you haven't seen me when I get all, oh, what's that modern expression, hyped up.''

"No," Shane said.

"You'll get used to it," Grandpa Joe said. "Andrew did, and Harry's adjusting well, too. I'm glad you came to work for me, Shane. This is a family company, and I enjoy having my family around me. When I die, which won't be soon, mind you, I'll leave this world knowing that what I built will be left in good, capable hands."

"I have to admit, I'm enjoying working here." Shane stiffened his spine as he saw the knowing gleam in his grandfather's eyes. "No, don't you even start gloating and telling me that you were right. I know you were. But I don't want to hear about it."

"Okay," Grandpa Joe said with a deep chuckle. "I won't tell you I was right about that. But I will tell you that I was right about Lindy. I was, wasn't I?"

Shane put the ultrasound picture back into his wallet. "Pretty much. She married me, didn't she?"

Grandpa Joe stroked his beard. "That she did. Although, I have to tell you, with your mother running the wedding, I was crossing my fingers that Lindy wouldn't run away. I know I would have."

Shane grinned. "I wasn't too worried. Knowing Mom, she would have just tracked Lindy down and guilted her to come back."

"True," Grandpa Joe acknowledged, with another knowing gleam in his blue eyes. "That's your mother. She definitely dances to her own drummer. But she fits Blake and makes him happy, so that's all that matters. I was quite worried about your father after his first wife's tragic death. He had Claire and the twins to consider. It was a dark time. And then he met Sara and..."

"She took over," Shane said, "and they had me."

"Well, in short, yes. She's definitely the driving force behind your father. But he loves Sara, and their relationship is blessed and really works. Speaking of relationships, how's yours and Lindy's doing? Now don't give me that look. Humor an old man. I only ask because I have a vested interest. I gave you the rules, you followed them, and she married you. She hasn't wanted out yet, has she?"

"No."

Grandpa Joe leaned forward. "You don't sound so sure."

"It's nothing like that," Shane said slowly. His mind raced. Should he tell? He couldn't keep the secret to himself, and Grandpa Joe did have a vested interest, like he'd said. "I think actually the opposite is occurring. I think she told me she loved me last night. I mean, I heard the words, but I don't know if she knew she was saying them. She was nearly asleep."

Grandpa Joe only said, "Oh."

"Oh is right. Now I don't know what to do, what to tell her. I mean, I have to tell her I heard the words."

Grandpa Joe got up and went to the minibar. He returned with two cans of soda and handed one of them to Shane. "Sorry. I forgot my manners. So tell me, what's so hard about that?"

Shane watched as Grandpa Joe popped the tab. "What's hard is that I can't say that I love her in return."

"Oh." Grandpa Joe took a long sip.

Shane set his unopened can of cola down on the coffee table. "Stop saying that. It's not helping. What I need is to know what to do. I mean, those words from a woman are like the kiss of death. Nothing is ever the same afterward, and Lindy and I have been getting along so well. I don't want to lose her over this. I don't want to hurt her, but I can't lie. We have fantastic sex. The best. She's beautiful. She's my best friend. She's having my baby. But that doesn't change the fact that I don't love her."

"You don't love her."

Shane shook his head. "No."

"No feelings for her whatsoever?"

Shane exhaled, his frustration obvious. "No. Not like that. You know I don't believe in that lovey-dovey nonsense. It's not real. It's a bunch of mumbo-jumbo corporations make up to sell candy and stuff."

Grandpa Joe didn't answer right away. Instead, he paused and turned toward the door. "Come in," he called.

But no one appeared.

Grandpa Joe rose to his feet. He made a quick glance heavenward. "This is carrying Johnny's orders a bit too far." He walked to the doorway.

"Is it the food?" Shane called when his grandfather didn't return right away.

Grandpa Joe turned around, and for the first time in Shane's entire life, he saw his grandfather look stricken. It was a terrifying sight, and immediately Shane knew something was very wrong. "It's Lindy. She's getting on the elevator. I think she overheard us."

"Oh God." Raw panic, unlike any he'd ever experienced, filled Shane. He jumped to his feet and raced to the door. Only his grandfather's arm across the door stopped him from exiting. "Let me pass. I have to go after her."

"No." The innate command in Grandpa Joe's voice froze Shane, and he tottered as his body got ahead of him. Shane stared at his grandfather, not believing he'd just heard the words.

"What do you mean, no?" Shane asked. He rebalanced himself and faced his grandfather. "I have to go after her."

Grandpa Joe didn't blink. "No. I said no because it's not a good idea."

Shane made a wild gesture. "Of course it is. She heard us! She might have heard what I said."

"And just what are you going to do if she did? Chase after her and tell her you didn't mean it? Tell her that you lied? Apologize for speaking the truth?"

"I—" Shane faltered. What had he done? "I didn't mean for her to hear me. It's cruel. I didn't want her hurt. I don't want to hurt her."

"I know you don't want to hurt her." The elevator

dinged, but this time it was a server carrying a tray from the executive cafeteria. "Come eat," Grandpa Joe said. "Food will help you think."

"Think? Eat? I can't do either right now. I need to stop her, to tell her—"

"Again, I ask you, to tell her what?" Grandpa Joe stood firm and guided Shane back to the sofa. I think you have a lot to think about. In fact, it seems to me that you may have pretty strong feelings for Lindy. I think you need to know exactly what they are before you go rushing off willy-nilly and make matters somehow even worse."

Shane watched the waiter put the food on a dining table. Despite seeing the covered plates, he had no appetite. "She's my best friend. I never meant to hurt her."

Grandpa Joe uncovered some carrot sticks. He waved one. "Do you love me?"

Shane leaned back against the sofa and ran an agitated hand through his hair. "What's that got to do with it? You're my grandfather. Of course I do."

"And your mother?" Grandpa Joe was having no problem eating, and he took a bite of raw carrot.

"Yes."

"Your father? Cousins?"

Was there a point to all this? Frustrated, Shane folded his hands together. "Yes. You're family."

Grandpa Joe stopped eating. "So why not Lindy? Lindy, the best thing that's ever happened to you. Lindy, who is having your baby. Lindy, who you describe as your best friend. Love isn't a feeling as much as it is a choice, Shane. You choose to let the feelings in, to let the feelings flow. You choose to care. So I ask you again, why can't you love Lindy?''

And with those words, Grandpa Joe reached over and removed a metal plate cover. ''They had the salmon sandwich.'' He brought the china plate over to Shane. Shane stared at the food. Although the sandwich looked delicious, he had completely lost his appetite. Not even the mouthwatering display could tempt him.

''I'm really not hungry,'' Shane said, his mind reeling at everything that had just been thrown at him in the last few minutes.

Grandpa Joe grabbed his own plate. ''Perhaps, but you'll eat it anyway. And while you do, I'm giving you an assignment.''

''I don't need work. I need to make amends with my wife.''

''That's what this assignment is about.'' Grandpa Joe picked up his fork and gestured at Shane to eat. ''Eat. And while you do, I want you to ponder the answer to my question. Why can't you love your wife?''

THANK GOD THEY hadn't seen her. That was the silver lining to all this, that and the fact that her secretary was away from her desk. Lindy brushed a tear away from her cheek as she stepped out onto her floor. All she had to do was grab her purse. To hell with working the rest of the day. They could dock her pay. Fire her for all she cared. Right now all she wanted to do was crawl into a hole and hide forever.

She'd known he didn't love her. But to actually hear him say it, that had cut like a knife. And he hadn't said it once; he'd said it several times. And each time, a part of her had died.

She couldn't take it anymore. Despite all Shane's promises, despite their phenomenal sex life, their perfect house, their perfect cars, despite that, the one ingredient that held it all together wasn't there. It never would be there. They lacked love.

Well, so much for Tina's advice. Worse, Tina hadn't even been available to talk. Lindy had left her a hysterical message, in essence saying that Shane didn't love her, and that he'd told his grandfather he never would.

So now there was no point in Lindy telling Shane how she felt. She'd heard that part of the conversation, too. He already knew she loved him. And he still didn't care. Lindy placed her hand protectively over her stomach as she pressed the button to get back on the elevator. She pushed it several times again, more in frustration with her situation than with the elevator being slow.

What was she going to do? She could stay and work at Jacobsen. She could stay and live with Shane and deal with the situation, the pain he'd put her through. No, she couldn't do either of those things.

Which left her nowhere except with massive decisions to make, decisions she didn't even know how to make or where to begin.

Lindy pressed her key fob, opening via remote the locks to her Grand Prix. Within moments she'd left the parking garage and pulled out onto Market Street, heading westbound toward the entrance to Interstate 64. She drummed her fingers on the steering wheel. The interstate entrance was just ahead, and once on that she could let the car loose.

Finally the light at Compton turned green. Lindy stepped on the accelerator and, as she drove into the intersection, there was the grinding sound of metal on metal and the world went black.

Chapter Ten

The voices in the warm blackness were distant and hazy. "She's unconscious." "Come on, sweetheart. Stay with us. The ambulance is on its way."

Another voice. Female. Hysterical. "He just ran the red light. Plowed right into her. Sent her spinning. Is she okay?"

A calmer voice. "Shh. She's getting the best care possible. This officer will take your statement."

Yet another voice. "Any ID?"

A female voice. "Yes. Her purse scattered on the floor." A rustling sound. "Here it is. Melinda Jean Brinks. Oh. Look at these."

"Ultrasound pictures."

"Let the paramedics know she might be pregnant. Ambulance is here."

More voices, each different, each the same, as various hands moved over her body. Something pricked, but in her haze Lindy felt but didn't feel the pain. Something firm encased her neck.

"Backboard ready."

In the blackness, Lindy felt herself lifted, something

hard slid underneath her. Something already covered her face. She tried to call Shane's name, but in the darkness, as her world slipped away, the words wouldn't come.

LESS THAN A MILE away, Shane sat in his office and gazed out the window. The view eastward down Market Street was beautiful. He tossed a tennis ball up into the air and caught it again. He could appreciate why Grandpa Joe chose this spot, with its phenomenal view of the Soldier's Memorial, Union Station, and even farther, Kiener Plaza, the Old Courthouse, and then the Gateway Arch.

Shane tossed the tennis ball one more time, catching it easily before putting it back into a drawer. His one-arm game of catch hadn't done anything to dispel his sense of disquiet.

He'd really screwed up this time.

"But do I love Lindy?" he asked aloud.

Damn, but he hated soul-searching.

Did he love Lindy? She was his best friend. She was his lover. She was the mother of his child. He'd vowed in front of God and witnesses to love her until death-do-us-part. But did he love her?

Of course he did. He loved her like his best friend. Like the mother of his child. Like his lover. He loved her like he'd love a member of his family.

Sure he loved her. And there, that answered Grandpa Joe's question.

If the question was really that simple.

For Shane knew it wasn't. Maybe it went back to

that Men are from Mercury or whatever-it-was-called
book. He could tell Lindy that he loved her and not
be lying.

But in doing so, he wouldn't be telling her the truth,
either, at least not the truth that she wanted to hear.
She wanted the endless devotion, the can't-live-
without-you, you're-the-only-one-for-me love. She
wanted that kind of declaration.

The kind Shane had given up on that summer when
he'd watched the girl press her hand up against the
bus window as it drove away.

After that summer he'd never loved anyone else in
the same way because he'd learned that love like that
wasn't real. It wasn't worth the pain, and even though
the pain eventually faded, the scar remained. He'd
learned that you didn't ever let people have the power
to hurt you, and, from that moment on, Shane hadn't
given anyone that power. People came into his life,
and then they left it, and he remained unscathed.

He didn't even worry much about the pain his partners might have felt. Perhaps that made him cold, distant, but he'd also learned that the pain went away for
everyone. It always did. He'd discovered that fact
when he'd dated women, called off the relationship,
and then seen them out with someone else less than a
week later. It was a mating game for the most eligible
partner, that's all dating was. He had simply been
Shane Jacobsen, rich, eligible catch who could make
a woman's life easy street.

"You're working late." Harry appeared in Shane's
doorway.

Shane swiveled around, away from the fantastic view. "So are you."

Harry stepped through the doorway. "Yeah, I guess. Megan had a doctor's appointment and then she was going to visit her mother for a while. Since this is one of those appointments she didn't want me at, I figured I could work a little bit later tonight. I had some things to get done, since I'm taking Friday off. There's a play in Chicago that Megan wants to see, so we're taking a minivacation to the Windy City this weekend."

"Oh." Shane picked up a pencil and rolled it between his fingers.

"Something wrong?"

Shane paused. "No, but I've got a question for you. It's something Lindy and I were talking about. If it's not too personal, how did you know you were in love with Megan?"

Harry grinned. "It's not too personal. And let me tell you, we hated each other at first. I couldn't believe it when Grandpa Joe made us work together. I thought I was getting a promotion and instead, there I was assigned to be her mentor."

Harry shook his head at the now fond memory. "I think I first knew I felt something for her besides just boss-to-employee interest, when one of the guys from the other firm asked her out. She went, and I was not happy about it. I think that's when I had to start answering those questions in my head. You know the ones, like why was she the only person occupying my thoughts, what little thing could I do to get her to notice me, what was she thinking about me, etc. I mean, she had a power over me. And when I hurt her, it devastated me. It felt like my world had ended. And at that moment I knew I didn't want to ever let her out of my life again. It was like that with you and Lindy, wasn't it?''

''Sort of,'' Shane said. ''She'd worked for me but I didn't see her until...'' His voice drifted off. Until the night of his party when she was the one he'd called. She was the one who had been missing, who hadn't been there. She was the one he'd wanted.

And when she had arrived he hadn't been able to leave her side. He'd introduced her as the love of his life. The painkillers and alcohol had freed what his heart always knew, and what his logical brain had kept hidden. He did love Lindy. With all his heart.

Love. True love. It really did exist in the adult world, and he'd found it. He'd had it with him all the time. It was a choice, and a feeling. It was the most freeing thing in the world, and the most petrifying. To hand someone your heart, that was the biggest leap of faith and trust that a man could take.

And he loved Lindy.

That's why he panicked when she'd been ill. That's why he'd brought her food when his mother had descended on her and read her the riot act. Love was why he hadn't wanted her to go to Jacobsen. Not because she was the best PA in the world, but because deep down he couldn't live his life without her.

And living without her was the scariest thought in the world. He loved her. He'd found her. He tried to conjure up the image of the girl on the bus, but he couldn't. It had disappeared. The only image he could see when he thought of the word *love*—that image was Lindy's.

"You look like you've seen a ghost," Harry said.

Shane stood up, his step suddenly unsteady. "I think I have," he said. He needed to find Lindy. Grandpa Joe had been right. Time had helped. He now knew what to say, how to make it all okay. "I'll walk you as far as the elevator."

But a quick look around Lindy's floor revealed that everyone had left for the evening. So Shane headed to the parking garage, and within moments revved the Corvette's engine as he backed out of the parking space. Although it was the start of a beautiful evening, he didn't waste time putting the convertible top down. He had to get home. He had to get to Lindy before she did anything foolish, like leave him before he told her he'd gotten a clue.

He pressed a button, putting on K-SHE-95, one of the nation's oldest rock stations. Heck, it was older than him. He watched as the car in front of him exited the parking garage, and then down the road a ways the light at Jefferson changed, meaning that Shane had to wait as several cars heading westbound passed him. Then he finally was clear to turn right.

The Rolling Stones song ended and Shane paused behind a long line of cars. Odd. The light at Compton must be malfunctioning. He turned up the volume as the traffic report began, announcing that the police were still clearing a two-car accident at Market and Compton.

Shane groaned. Great. He had to get to Lindy and he couldn't even get to the interstate quickly. The car in front of him moved up twenty feet, and Shane followed suit. It took him thirty minutes to travel what would normally take him a maximum of five.

He finally approached the intersection. Lights danced from the top of three police cars, and he could see the flash of an ambulance as it pulled away. Two policemen directed traffic as one huge flatbed tow truck loaded a foreign sports car with a destroyed front end. The other flatbed was maneuvering into position to move a—

Bile rose in Shane's throat as a terrible panic filled him. Bronze Grand Prix GTPs were a dime a dozen. But despite the crushed driver's side door that veered repulsively inward, this Grand Prix looked all too familiar. And this was the way Lindy drove home every day.

Ignoring the irritated beeping of the car horn behind him, Shane pulled the wheel to the right, parked the Corvette illegally in a nondriving lane and got out. Insane fear overwhelmed him as he ran up to the Grand Prix.

"Hey, buddy, I gotta move this car," the tow-truck driver said.

"Just a minute." Shane looked inside, seeing but not seeing the items strewn about. Already a policeman was yelling at him to leave the scene.

"Lindy," Shane said. As if he'd been told, he knew. He turned to the tow-truck driver. "This is my wife's car."

"Sorry," the man said. He looked flustered. "I've got to clear the intersection."

A policeman approached. "This is my wife's car," Shane said with an erratic point as the Grand Prix was hoisted away. "Where's my wife?"

The policeman tried to calm Shane down, but he'd have none of it. "Where is she? What happened? Is she all right?" Shane craned his head, searching the area for a sign of Lindy. He couldn't find her.

The policeman somehow guided Shane out of the roadway. "What's your wife's name?"

"Lindy." Shane swallowed. "Melinda. Lindy for short. What happened here? Where's my wife?"

The policeman nodded and put out his hands in a comforting gesture. "She was broadsided. She's been taken to the emergency room at St. Louis University Medical Center. There's a police officer with your wife and the officer will have some further questions..."

But Shane didn't wait for more. Lindy was at the hospital. He ran back toward the Corvette. St. Louis University Medical Center, or SLU as the natives called it, was less than two miles away. Not knowing Lindy's condition, he didn't have a single moment to lose.

As THE AUTOMATIC DOORS to the emergency room burst open, all eyes turned toward Shane's running figure. He paid little attention to the people sitting in the waiting room and instead rushed up to the nurse's window.

"Lindy Jacobsen," he said. Shane caught his breath as the woman blinked at him. "Melinda Brinks. Came in from a car accident at Compton and Market. I'm her husband. Where is she? How is she?"

"Just a moment, sir."

The admitting nurse ignored Shane's craning neck as he tried to look past her and see the patient rooms, see anything. But there was nothing to see, and again panic began to claim Shane's senses. "She is here, isn't she?"

The nurse typed something into the computer before glancing back up at him. "Yes. Calm down. Let me contact one of the nurses and tell her that you're here. If you could just take a seat for me." The nurse stood up and gestured toward the waiting area.

"I don't want a seat! I want my wife. She could be dying and—"

"Sir," The nurse took a step back. "It'll just be a moment. Please have a seat."

But Shane couldn't sit. Ignoring the interested or sympathetic stares of the onlookers, he paced. The moment the nurse promised seemed to stretch forever. Finally the nurse returned and Shane rushed up to the counter. "Well?" he demanded.

"Mr. Brinks?"

Shane turned as the door into the emergency room inner sanctum opened. A nurse in green scrubs stood there, and Shane turned toward her. "I'm Shane Jacobsen. Lindy Brinks is my wife."

The nurse didn't smile. "Sorry. Mr. Jacobsen, if you'll please follow me."

Shane followed the nurse into the E.R. "How is she?"

"Stable," the nurse replied. She stopped outside a room. "She's in here. Doctor Jones will be with you in just a moment."

Shane stepped into the room and saw her instantly. He'd been wrong this morning. Now he knew true fear. Never before had he seen anyone so pale or so lifeless, and this was Lindy, the woman he loved.

She lay so still, and it took Shane a long moment to finally see the shallow rise and fall of her chest. An IV tube extended from her left wrist to a plastic bag filled with some kind of fluid hanging from a silver pole. A line on a nearby monitor rose and fell, and as Shane watched the movement, he had no idea if Lindy's heartbeat was regular or not. He twisted his hands together. Never had he felt so helpless. "Lindy, I'm so sorry," he whispered.

The nurse made a notation on the chart and, as she made a movement toward the door, the doctor stepped in.

"Mr. Brinks?"

"Jacobsen," Shane corrected. "I'm Shane Jacobsen. Lindy and I married in July."

"Sorry." The doctor turned to the nurse, and they exchanged some quick words that, because of the medical jargon, Shane didn't understand.

"How's my wife?" Shane said as the nurse left.

"Stable." Some men in white moved into the room.

Shane's eyes widened as the men began to move Lindy's hospital bed. "What's going on?"

The doctor's tone remained patient and calm. "As your wife has not yet regained consciousness, we're sending her for a CT scan." Lindy disappeared from view, and Shane focused on what the doctor was saying. "We've already run several basic tests such as X-rays, blood tests and a urine test. There was no blood in the urine, which is a good sign, and she is definitely pregnant."

"Of course she's pregnant," Shane said. "She just had her ultrasound done yesterday."

The doctor nodded. "Yes, but you weren't here yet and we couldn't just assume she was pregnant because of ultrasound pictures. The pictures could have belonged to a friend."

"Oh." Shane had never felt so far out of his depth. "So will she be okay?"

"The CT scan will give us more information as to what is occurring inside her skull. From it, we will be able to determine if she has any internal injuries such as bruising or bleeding."

Shane paced. "And what if—"

The doctor politely cut Shane off. "Let's not speculate until we know what we're dealing with. Trust me, she's receiving the best possible medical care. Our E.R. isn't very busy right now, and as a full level-one trauma center, we have every service available. But we do need some further information. Ah, here's Sheila. She has some questions for you." The doctor stepped toward the door. "I will be back as soon as your wife returns from her CT scan."

The next forty-five minutes seemed to be some of

the longest of Shane's life. Not only did he get Lindy fully admitted to the E.R. and her health insurance information straightened out, but also Shane had attempted to answer dozens of medical questions that he really didn't have an answer for. While he did know the name of Lindy's obstetrician, he didn't know any of her family medical history.

In addition, a police officer had stopped by and gotten more information regarding Lindy's automobile insurance and her contact information. While the officer didn't fill Shane in on any accident details, Shane was now in possession of Lindy's purse and the fact that the car had been taken to the towing company's lot.

Finally the hospital staff wheeled Lindy back into the room. Immediately Shane saw that she remained unconscious. Not knowing what to do was the most helpless feeling in the world. He had to do something. Shane reached over and gently clasped Lindy's hand in his. Isn't that what those medical shows always advised? Talking to the loved one? Letting the patient know you were there?

"Hey, Lindy," Shane said. "I'm here."

He fell silent. What else was he supposed to say? He drew a breath, paused, and for once let his heart talk.

"Lindy, I know you probably can't hear me, but I have to tell you that I've been a fool. But you probably know that. You've put up with me long enough to know how dense I am. But right now I just want you to believe me when I tell you that I realized I do love you. God, Lindy, I truly love you. I'm so sorry that you overheard what I said to my grandfather. I was an idiot and I am truly sorry. Forgive me, honey. I love you.''

But Lindy remained silent. A nurse came in and again checked on Lindy. The nurse gave Shane a comforting smile. ''Her CT scans are back. Dr. Jones will be right in to talk to you.''

Was that the doctor's name? It had been stitched in blue on his white coat, but concerned about Lindy, Shane hadn't paid enough attention to remember it.

Ten minutes later, Dr. Jones reappeared. ''Mr. Jacobsen.'' Shane turned and let the doctor pass.

The doctor walked over to Lindy, looked her over, and checked her chart again. Then he turned to Shane. ''Unfortunately, the CT scan didn't come back negative.'' The doctor paused for a split second as he made a notation, and Shane stopped himself from interrupting. ''A negative CT scan would have meant that Melinda...''

Shane couldn't help himself. ''Lindy,'' he corrected.

''Lindy,'' the doctor repeated. ''A negative scan would have meant that she had a simple concussion and should then be regaining consciousness within minutes to a few hours after the impact. However, her CT scan showed some bruising, which means she has a moderate to severe concussion. The type of injury she has is called a contre-coup injury.''

The medical word meant nothing to Shane. ''A what?''

''A contre-coup injury,'' the doctor repeated. ''This

means that the bruising is actually on the opposite side from the impact, so the bruising is on the right side of her head.''

Shane ran an agitated hand through his hair. ''I don't understand. The police said the other driver hit her on her driver-side door. In essence, he T-boned her.''

The doctor nodded as if this all made perfect sense to him. ''Yes. That means the car is pushed to Lindy's right, forcing her head to the left. Since the brain floats in a fluid, after it hits the left side of the skull, it gets sloshed back to the right and hits that side of the skull, too.''

He glanced at Shane, as if making sure he was following. ''That causes bruising on both sides, which means a more severe injury. The good news, though, is that the CT scan does not show any evidence of subdural hematoma.''

Shane was confused. ''What?''

''Subdural hematoma. This refers to bleeding inside the head. This would have required a neurosurgeon to come in and drill a burr-hole to release the pressure before it causes brain damage. So, while your wife is in serious condition, to use layman's terms, it could have been much worse.''

With his arms at his sides, Shane made tight fists and then stretched his fingers in an attempt to reduce stress. None of this medical jargon made much sense, and the biggest question Shane had hadn't been answered. ''So what goes on from here? When is she going to wake up? What are you going to be doing for her?''

"Right now she's stable, breathing on her own, and we're monitoring her closely. This kind of an injury can put her out for a couple hours or even overnight. She's being admitted to the ICU where we can give her the best care possible. When she wakes up, we'll take it from there.''

Disbelief filled Shane. "So we wait? That's it? That's all?''

The doctor nodded. "I know that's not the answer you wanted to hear, but yes, that's all. The human body is a pretty remarkable thing. Her being unconscious is actually part of how her body is healing itself from the trauma of the accident. Mr. Jacobsen, I know this is the hardest part for family members to deal with. But right now, we wait. In just a few minutes we'll move her to the ICU.''

Shane nodded, and, as his knees suddenly weakened, he lowered himself back into the black plastic chair next to Lindy's bed.

Right now they had to wait.

He reached for her hand again and lowered his forehead so that it rested on his forearm. For the first time since he was seven, Shane wept.

Chapter Eleven

His neck hurt. As Shane woke up, he raised his head, moving it first to the left and then to the right to try and work out the kink. Although the stretching helped, it didn't erase his discomfort.

He glanced at Lindy. He'd remained in the ICU with her all night, when he could, dozing on and off in the hard chair next to her bed. Every time he'd checked on her, her eyes remained closed and her breathing steady. The IV dripped and the machine monitoring Lindy's blood pressure, pulse and respiratory rate did its thing. Shane checked his watch. Lindy was still unconscious and it was now 9:00 a.m.

Shane exhaled slowly. The worry that he'd managed to push off during brief intervals of light sleep had returned with a vengeance. These last few hours had been the longest hours of his life.

A nurse entered the room, this time a different person from the previous evening. The shifts must have changed while Shane had been asleep.

"Good morning," the nurse said as she lifted Lindy's eyelids to check her pupils. Last night, when the nurse had done this, Shane had asked what was going on. He'd gotten the answer that Lindy was receiving what would be frequent neuro checks.

"We're looking to see if her pupils are equal in size and how they react to light," the nurse had said. "Unequal or sluggish pupils could indicate a problem."

Now Shane remained silent as the nurse finished the neuro checks and then examined the machines. She turned to him before she left the room.

"There's coffee in the waiting room," she offered.

"Thanks," Shane said. His body ached for some caffeine and some food, but he ignored the annoying grumble of his stomach. He couldn't leave Lindy. No matter what, and no matter how his stomach affected him, she was more important. She couldn't wake up alone.

"Shane."

Shane turned upon hearing the sound of his father's voice. Blake Jacobsen filled the doorway to Lindy's ICU room, and Shane was glad to see him. "Dad. Hey. Thanks for coming. How'd you know?"

Blake Jacobsen entered the small hospital room, his treasured Bible in his right hand. "Your grandfather notified everyone after you called him early this morning. He said that he volunteered to let everyone know what's happened. So how's she doing? Any change?"

Shane looked back at Lindy, mentally willing her to wake up. He held her hand. Her eyes remained closed. "She's stable and they keep checking on her but so far there's no change."

"I'm sorry," Blake said. He sat down in the room's other chair.

"So am I," Shane said. He played with Lindy's fingertips but she didn't respond. How much he wanted her to react, to do something, anything! Shane took a deep breath. "I'm worried, Dad. She needs to come around. I said some terrible things that I didn't mean for her to overhear. I haven't been able to apologize, to retract them. I want her to know I didn't mean them."

Blake nodded, the nod of a man used to hearing people's personal confessions. "It always seems to work that way. Why is it that we never tell people how we feel about them? For some reason, showing our natural human emotions is considered a weakness. We're afraid it gives people power over us, something to use against us, something to hurt us with. So too often we wait until it's too late."

Blake's Jacobsen-blue eyes clouded as a memory returned, and his fingers gripped the Bible a little tighter. "I did that with Kristina and—" he drew a sharp breath "—to an extent, I've made that exact same mistake with you."

At that admission, Blake scooted the plastic chair over and took a seat next to Shane and near Lindy's bedside. He reached out and placed a comforting hand on his son's shoulder. "As soon as Lindy wakes up, you be sure to tell her how you feel. Apologize. Kiss her. Hug her if they'll let you. Right now don't worry about things you have no control over. Those things take care of themselves. But you make sure she knows that you never want to almost lose her again." Blake looked at Lindy. "I assume the baby's okay?"

His father removed his hand and it amazed Shane how effective his touch had been. The world seemed a bit brighter. "Her obstetrician came earlier this morning. Everything's fine."

Pure relief crossed his father's face. "Good. Your mother and I were worried about that. Speaking of, your mother will be in later to check on you. Since it's the ICU, we decided to come in shifts."

Shane reached forward and stroked Lindy's forehead. "Don't you have a plane to catch? I thought you had to pack? Don't you have revivals on the West Coast?"

Blake shook his head, his peppery gray hair too short to fall into his eyes. "We pushed our flight back a day."

A silence fell between the men as Shane realized the implications of that. For once, his needs had come first. His parents had rearranged their schedule so that they could be there for him. His father had come to the ICU to simply be by Shane's side. His father was here. It so overpowered him that "Thanks" was all he could manage.

"So how are you holding up?" his dad asked.

Shane toyed with Lindy's fingers again. She loved it when he played with her fingers, and he again mentally willed her to move. But she remained still. "I'm fine."

"Which means that you haven't slept much, eaten

anything, or left her bedside for a moment,'' Blake observed with a sympathetic smile.

"Right," Shane admitted.

Blake rested his Bible on his left knee. "I tell you what, why don't you go to the lounge and get some coffee, or better yet, go to the cafeteria and get yourself something to eat."

Shane looked at his father to see if he was actually serious. Seeing that Blake was, Shane panicked. "I can't do that. What if she wakes up?"

"I'll be here," Blake said. He patted his Bible with a simple, quiet authority. "Besides, it'll give me some time alone to pray over her. Unless you'd like to stay, too."

"I—" Shane said, and then his voice faltered. At that moment he had never admired his father more, and Shane took a good hard look at him. His father had turned sixty-five that year. Lines creased his forehead and crow's feet cornered his eyes and lips. But on Blake's countenance rested an inner peace that Shane had never had. His father was indeed blessed. Shane stood. "I think I'll take you up on your offer. I could use some food and freshening up."

"A good idea."

"I'm glad you're here," he told his father.

His father caught Shane's hand for a moment. Both men's Jacobsen blues locked gazes. "I'm always here, son. Even when I forget what's important, that doesn't change how I feel. Always know that you are right here. Always right here."

Taking their linked hands, Blake touched his heart.

Then he broke the connection and freed Shane's hand. "Now go get yourself something to eat. Take your time. Let me have a little talk with the Man upstairs to see what he can do."

"I'll have a little talk later with Him, too," Shane said.

Blake nodded and opened the Bible to the New Testament. "A very good idea. I'm sure He'd love to hear from you and there's a chapel on the way back from the cafeteria if you don't want to chance Lindy overhearing anything personal. Now go get some food in your body. The last thing you need would be to pass out from dehydration or malnutrition or whatever it is when Lindy finally wakes up."

"True." Still standing, Shane stretched out some of his aching limbs before moving toward the door. He turned back to face his father one last time, the obvious written on his face.

"I'll send for you if she wakes up," Blake said, answering Shane's silent plea.

"Thanks."

But even two hours later, when Blake finally left the ICU, Lindy remained unconscious. Shane glanced at his watch. Twelve-fifteen. He rested his elbows on his knees and put his head in his hands, weaving his fingers into the blond locks around his ears. He needed a haircut. Worse, he needed a shave. Even though his father would have waited while he shaved, Shane hadn't wanted to be away from Lindy any longer. Another nurse came and went, smiling sympathetically as she checked the machine and performed the tests that were now routine.

Shane glanced at his watch again. Thirty-eight minutes after twelve. Time certainly wasn't flying. He dropped his head into his hands again and closed his eyes.

Although not soundly, he slept.

A slight rustling sound woke him, and not recognizing it, Shane frowned. Blinking, he raised his head. Lindy's arm was moving, her fingers sliding across the bed sheet as if feeling its texture.

Sleepiness vanished and Shane jumped to his feet and leaned over Lindy. Her eyelids fluttered softly, as if trying to open but instead finding the light too harsh. Her lips attempted a word.

"Lindy!" Shane calmed his voice. "Hey, Lindy. I'm right here, my darling. Lindy, can you hear me?"

Her eyelids fluttered open, and she blinked rapidly as she tried to adjust to her surroundings. "Shh…"

She was calling his name, and he moved so that she could see him. His new body position also blocked some of the overhead light. "I'm right here, Lindy. I'm here."

Hope continued to fill him even though her eyelids fluttered closed again. A nurse came into the room. "She's coming around," Shane said.

"Wonderful," the nurse said, and Shane watched as the nurse did a quick exam before making a note of the time on her chart. "I'll get her doctor."

"Shane." The full word finally escaped from Lindy's lips.

"I'm here." Now that the nurse was out of the way, Shane leaned over and stroked Lindy's forehead. He took her hand in his. Her brown eyes opened fully and she stared up at him. "Hey, gorgeous. Did I ever tell you how beautiful your eyes are?"

With her eyes wide she looked like a doe caught in the headlights, but to Shane Lindy had never been more beautiful. "What happened? Where am I? I hurt."

Shane pushed her hair back away from her face and stroked her forehead. "Hey, honey. I know you hurt. You're at St. Louis University medical center. You were in a car accident and have been unconscious since last night."

"Oh," Lindy said. She closed her eyes again for a brief moment. She opened them again, as if the thought had just registered. "A car accident?"

"Yes," he said. Lindy frowned, her brow furrowing into lines that immediately caused Shane worry. "What's wrong?" he asked.

Her voice was one notch above a whisper. "I don't remember."

At first Shane barely comprehended what she'd said. "You don't remember? You don't remember the accident?"

"No." Lindy tried to turn her head but winced instead. "My head hurts."

"Stay still," Shane soothed. "You have internal bruising. That's why you've been unconscious."

"The baby…"

"The baby's fine," Shane answered her. A doctor

entered the room. He smiled at Lindy. "Hello, Lindy, I'm Doctor Wheeler. It's good to finally have you awake." He moved over to Lindy's bedside. "Now let me get a look at you."

Shane watched as the doctor checked Lindy's chart and then talked to her so that he could assess her level of alertness. "She doesn't remember the accident," Shane said.

The doctor didn't look too surprised. "That's not unusual." He smiled at Lindy. "What's the last thing you remember?"

"Driving to work," Lindy said. She winced again, as if trying to recall the memory hurt.

"But you know this guy here?"

"He's my husband."

"Well, that's good because that's what he's been telling us. We wouldn't want some strange man in here." The doctor grinned at his joke. "Well, Lindy, it seems like you have a case of retrograde amnesia. This can be fairly common with the type of head trauma you incurred. In most cases, full memory returns, although it'd only be a guess to say how long yours might take."

The doctor then proceeded to ask Lindy a few more questions. Shane watched as she correctly identified the President of the United States, where she worked, where she'd gone to high school, and the name of her best friend. The questions confirmed that her memory was only missing the events of the day of the accident.

The doctor made a notation on the chart. "You'll be in the ICU for a few more hours and then we'll transfer you to a med/surg floor for observation. The good news is that while you'll still be monitored, the nurses won't have to poke and prod at you as much. Now, if all goes well, we'll be able to send you home in one to two days.''

The moment the doctor left the room, Shane took Lindy's hand in his like he'd been doing all day. The moment had finally arrived. He took a deep breath. ''There's something I need to tell you,'' he said.

Lindy looked at him expectantly.

''I love you,'' Shane said. Her mouth fell open slightly, but before she could speak the door to Lindy's room opened. ''Time to remove your catheter,'' a nurse said, ''and freshen you up.''

THE NURSE'S INTERRUPTION was as welcome as it was unwelcome. Having a few less things stuck in her body was a good thing, but yet the nurse's arrival prevented any further conversation with Shane.

Shane loved her? Since when? The thought had been consuming her since she'd said the words and Lindy tried to concentrate on Shane's earnest declaration as the hospital staff moved her to a gurney and then wheeled her toward the elevators.

She wished her memory wasn't so black. Shane loved her?

He'd been telling her ever since she'd come around, but instinctively Lindy knew something wasn't right.

But what wasn't right about it escaped her. She knew that the near death of loved ones often made people confess things that normally they wouldn't confess. But Lindy remembered that she'd gone to bed saying she loved Shane, but that he hadn't returned the words. Perhaps her accident had made him realize that he needed to say the words out loud. But concentration for too long hurt, and Lindy let the thought drift away as the hospital staff transferred her to a new bed on a med-surg floor.

Shane was beside her immediately. "Hey," he said. "Comfortable?"

She smiled at him. He certainly did look loving, and she'd waited to see that look on his face for far too long. "As good as it gets."

"Can I adjust anything? Plump anything?"

He was so sweet that despite her headache, Lindy felt better. "No."

He planted a kiss on her forehead. "You heard what I said, didn't you?"

"Every time you've said it," Lindy said.

"Good. You'll be hearing it often."

"I'd like that," Lindy said. She couldn't help but smile at him. He did look so scruffy with his face unshaven and his shirtsleeves rolled up. Before she'd left the ICU, the nurse who had helped her to the bathroom had told Lindy that Shane had been there all night. He'd been so sweet to stay with her, so devoted.

"My father visited earlier. He gave good advice. They pushed their trip back to be with me."

Lindy had enough of a memory to know how important that was to Shane. "I'm glad."

"I was so worried about you," Shane said.

"I know," Lindy said, for somehow she did know.

But at that moment, Grandpa Joe and Henrietta arrived and any further conversation with Shane had to wait.

But by the time Grandpa Joe and Henrietta left, Lindy had tired. Shane kissed her good-night, told her that he loved her, and Lindy drifted off into a contented sleep knowing that should she awaken, he'd be right there in the chair beside her bed.

"I'M TIRED of hospital food," Lindy said the next afternoon as she spooned a bite of green gelatin into her mouth. At least lime-flavored was her favorite, and the chicken broth hadn't been too tasteless.

Shane grinned at her. "Well, if all goes well, you get to leave tomorrow. At home Marni will fix you all your favorites."

"Home," Lindy said. She leaned back against her pillow. "That would be nice. And I've got to get back to work. I've missed so much."

Shane shook his head. "Work doesn't matter. You're to follow the doctor's orders, and if he says to rest, that's exactly what you are going to do. You have to let your bruising heal."

"Yes, boss," Lindy said. "And maybe I'll get my memory back." Even though her head didn't ache as much, her memory still hadn't returned, even after Shane had described her day to her.

"You had lunch with Tina, worked, and went home," he had said. "The man broadsided you." But even his explanation hadn't jogged her missing memory into returning.

But actually, she didn't care. Shane loved her. He'd

told her he'd realized it the day after their lovemaking, that was when he'd figured it out.

"Lindy!"

Lindy glanced at the doorway. Tina stood there, a big green potted plant in her hands. "I just got the message. I've been in Las Vegas. We had a layover and so a group of us stayed to gamble. How are you? Oh, dumb question. Lindy! I've been so worried about you! As soon as I got home I got the message and I—" Tina stopped midstream, as if realizing she was babbling.

Lindy pushed the rolling bedside table away. "I'm better. Come and talk to me. Thanks for the plant."

"Yeah, well it's tacky to come to these places empty-handed."

Tina's nervousness showed and Lindy made a gesture. "You can put the plant over on the windowsill with all the others. I've got quite a collection. Everyone in Shane's family sent something."

Tina suddenly seemed to notice Shane. She stared at him. "Hello, Shane," Tina said as she put her plant down.

"Tina," Shane acknowledged.

Feeling the evident tension between the two, Lindy gave Shane her best beguiling smile. "Shane, be a dear and see if the gift shop or cafeteria is open. I'd love some Ho Ho's and as of today, no one said I can't eat what I want."

Shane stared at her. "You want Ho Ho's?"

Lindy patted her stomach. "The baby does. He was deprived of chocolate while I was unconscious."

"Ho Ho's," Shane repeated. "If that's really what you want."

"I do."

Shane came and kissed Lindy on the forehead. She noticed that he didn't look too happy about being dismissed. "I'll be right back," he said.

"Okay." She watched him leave before she spoke to Tina. "There. I've sent him away so we can have a few minutes alone."

"You didn't have to do that," Tina said. She sat down in the chair Shane had vacated.

Lindy sighed. "Yes, I did. You know, one of these days I hope the two of you can both get along."

Tina fingered the hem of her shorts. "We might, when he finally treats you right."

Lindy's expression turned quizzical. "What do you mean, treats me right? He's been so sweet to me through all this. Before his mother flew out West this afternoon, she came by and told me that Shane hasn't left the hospital since the accident happened. She confirmed what the nurse told me."

Tina looked skeptical, and for a moment she refused to meet Lindy's gaze. Finally she looked up. "Okay, maybe he does really care for you. Maybe it's not just guilt."

Lindy's headache began to return. Tina's words hurt. Lindy rubbed her temples. "Of course Shane cares. He's even told me he loves me. In fact, he won't stop saying it."

"He loves you? But that's impossible! I mean, I've

heard of accidents bringing out the true feelings of people, but he was so insistent.''

Lindy adjusted her blanket. ''Tina, what are you talking about?''

Tina leaned forward, her worry evident. ''Lindy, don't you remember? We met the day of the accident because you'd told Shane you loved him and he didn't say the words back. You were quite distraught about the whole thing.''

''Oh.'' Lindy rubbed her temples again. The pain was sharpening. ''Actually, I don't remember even having lunch with you. My memory of everything between driving to work that day to waking up in the ICU is totally gone. The doctor called it retrograde amnesia. He says I'll get my memory back, but he isn't sure exactly when. No one is, except that it should be soon.''

Tina stood and came over to Lindy's bedside. ''Lindy, I'm so sorry. I didn't know. And I didn't mean to upset you.''

Although her head still hurt, Lindy managed a smile. ''I'm not upset. My head's starting to hurt for some reason. That's all.''

''I should go get a nurse.''

''No. My headaches come and go. I have bruising on my brain or something like that. It's a term I can't pronounce. Anyway, I'm still a little fuzzy about everything the doctor explained to me, but Shane can tell you. He's got it down pat.''

''So he's really been here the whole time?'' Lindy noticed a bit of awe in Tina's voice.

"All of it. I think my having the accident made him realize how much I really mean to him."

Tina managed a smile. "A knock on *his* head would have been easier than you getting one on yours."

"True. But he loves me." Lindy's head now really pounded. Maybe she should call the nurse. Something was wrong.

Tina gripped Lindy's hand. "I shouldn't be a nay-sayer, not at a time like this. I'm sorry. If you're sure he loves you, then I'll be sure, too."

The pounding in Lindy's head was excruciating. She'd waited for Shane to love her. So why was she questioning it? Was it not her dream come true? And Shane certainly had looked earnest enough. She'd seen an emotion in his eyes that she knew hadn't been there before she'd woken up in the hospital. Tina knew more than she was telling, and Lindy wanted to know what it was. "Tina, men change their minds. Tell me, why aren't you sure?"

Tina shook her head. "It's nothing."

"No, tell me. You're my best friend. You must tell me."

"Lindy, I—"

"Please," Lindy pleaded. She winced. How long had it been since her last pain medication? Just a few moments more and she'd call for a nurse. Just as soon as Tina told her everything.

Tina tightened her grip. "You've paled. Are you sure you're okay?"

She wasn't, but she couldn't allow Tina to digress. "Yes. Tell me."

Tina took a deep breath. "After we met for lunch, I went to an afternoon movie with Tom. I'd turned my phone off, and while I was there, you left me a hysterical message on my voice mail asking me to call you. You said Shane didn't love you, and you'd overheard him telling his grandfather several times that he never would."

And upon hearing Tina's words, Lindy's missing memory roared back.

WHEN SHANE STEPPED out of the elevator, the first thing he noticed was the flurry of activity near Lindy's doorway. Tina stood outside of it, and from thirty feet Shane could clearly see that she was shaken.

Shane cleared the distance down the hallway in two seconds. He craned his head over Tina's shoulder. He could see a doctor examining Lindy. "What's wrong?"

Tina gazed at Shane, her expression bitter. Her look chilled him. "She just got her memory back."

Shane's full weight came down upon his feet and he stared at Tina. "Her memory's back?"

Tina crossed her arms over her chest. The shaking was gone, and in its place was a controlled fury. "Yes, all of it came back. Including the fact that you swore to your grandfather that you don't love her."

The package of Ho Ho's slipped through Shane's hand, but he didn't bend to retrieve it from the tile floor. "It was all a mistake. I did some thinking and—"

Tina drew herself up, her voice forceful, yet still a

low, for-his-ears-only sound. "You're the reason she ran away from the office. Did you know she left me a hysterical message on my voice mail? She said she couldn't even stand being in the same office, that she needed time to think. I can't even begin to forgive you for hurting her. Do you know how much that woman loves you? You are the biggest fool in the world, Shane Jacobsen."

"Not anymore." Shane broke eye contact and he reached down for Lindy's package of chocolate cakes. He stood back up, his posture sure. "I love her, and I knew it before the accident happened. I'm going to make everything okay."

Tina still blocked the doorway, as if refusing to let him pass. Her eyes narrowed. "You need to see that you do. Lindy means the world to me, and I'm not going to stand by and let you hurt her. She's had enough of that in her life. For the last three years she hasn't even been able to date anyone because of you. Because she'd fallen in love with you. You, and you don't even deserve her."

Shane tilted his head slightly. "You're never going to like me, are you?"

"No."

Shane pursed his lips. At least Tina was honest. "Hopefully someday I'll be able to change your mind. You're Lindy's best friend, and she's my wife. From now forward, she'll know it, too."

As if recognizing the conviction in Shane's words, Tina nodded slightly. "Make her happy, Shane. That's all I want for her."

"I will," Shane promised.

The doctor came to the doorway, forcing both of them to step aside in order to let him leave the room. "Mr. Jacobsen," the doctor said. "Your wife has regained her memory. I've done some checks, and everything, including your wife's headache, is normal. We're planning on keeping her overnight, and if she continues to make good progress, she might be able to go home tomorrow evening."

Elation filled Shane. "That's good news," he said.

"Very good," the doctor said with a nod. "Your wife is a fortunate woman. She could have been injured much worse, but she and the baby are both doing fine."

"Thank you," Shane said. Ignoring Tina, he entered the room. He knew leaving Tina in the hall was rude, but right now he wanted to see Lindy. He wanted to talk to her, to hug and kiss her just the way his father had suggested.

The bed was up at a small, less-than-45-degree angle, and her eyes were closed when he approached. "Lindy," he said. He set the package of Hostess Ho Ho's on the rolling table.

Her long eyelashes fluttered open, revealing those brown eyes he loved so much. He had so much to tell her, so much to make up to her. She blinked. "Shane."

Emotional pain in her voice, and he knew he'd caused it. Remaining standing, he bent over her. "I heard the news," he said. "You might get to go home tomorrow night."

"She has a huge headache," Tina reminded him as she stepped into the room. Shane straightened and glared at Lindy's friend. Tina ignored him. "Lindy, love, I'm going to get going, but I didn't want to leave without saying goodbye. I'll come by your house in a few days."

Tina leaned down and gave Lindy a quick kiss on her cheek. "I love you like a sister, Lindy. You let me know if you need me."

"I will," Lindy said.

As Shane watched the exchange, it all suddenly became clear. The love of two best friends permeated the room, and Shane suddenly understood. No wonder he and Tina were such adversaries. Tina saw him as the enemy. Well, not anymore, Shane resolved. He loved Lindy. He would spend the rest of his days making it up to her, telling her. Starting now.

He reached forward, moving a lock of stray blond hair out of her face. "Are you up for talking?"

"I don't know," Lindy said. "My head's pounding. They gave me something for it, but it hasn't kicked in."

"We can talk later," Shane said.

"Is there a later?" Lindy asked. Shane winced. He deserved that. He hated the pain he saw in her eyes, but he knew that right now wasn't the time for professing his love. She wouldn't believe him. Not after what he'd said, what he'd done. They needed to talk first.

But he could offer her reassurance. He nodded. "There is a later for us, Lindy. There's a future, too." He took a deep breath and took her hand in his. "We have a future. That I promise you."

Chapter Twelve

"Welcome home, miss. Are you sure you should be walking?" Marni bustled about, and Lindy gave her an appreciative smile.

"I'm fine," Lindy said. Seeing Marni's dubious expression, she added, "Really. I practised walking at the hospital before I left. They wanted to make sure I didn't get dizzy or anything."

Marni didn't look convinced. "If you're sure, miss. Now anything you need, you just tell me."

"We have flowers and plants in the car," Shane said.

"Oh, very good." Marni moved toward the garage, grateful for something to do.

"That should keep her busy for a bit," Shane said. "She seemed like she needed a task."

"People often do," Lindy agreed. "It makes them feel less helpless."

Shane reached out a hand to steady her. He gently cupped her elbow and warmth traveled to her toes before he released her. "Got it?"

"Yes." Lindy took another unassisted step forward.

Shane had wanted to carry her, but she hadn't wanted to be back in his arms. Not yet.

She stared at her husband. After Tina left, they'd done little talking, as Shane's sisters had visited. This morning she hadn't seen much of him because after Grandpa Joe had arrived at 9:00 a.m., Shane had finally left the hospital and gone home. He'd showered, changed, and when he'd returned a few hours later he'd swapped out his Corvette for the family sedan that was now loaded down with the flowers and plants she received during her stay.

Dressed in his casual shorts and polo shirt, Shane had never looked sexier. But sex was not on her release paperwork. That was definitely out for a while. Besides, Lindy rationalized, how pathetic was she? She had to admit to herself that she wanted to make love to a man that, despite his professions otherwise, probably didn't love her back. Had she really stooped so low that she'd stay with Shane under any circumstances, even now?

Lindy took another slow step forward. There wasn't anything wrong with her nervous system, but she wanted to make sure she didn't fall.

"I still think I should carry you," Shane said.

"I'm fine," Lindy said. "I'm an independent woman. I want to walk on my own."

"I know you're an independent woman. That's always been one of the things I've admired about you, Lindy. But the doctors said not to overdo it. You need your rest. You can walk later. As it is, you'll need physical therapy to help your muscles loosen from the impact.''

''I know,'' Lindy said. She paused at the base of the stairs. Walking was tiring, and there was no way she wanted to try the steps. She turned to her husband. ''Okay, you can carry me.''

He scooped her up into his arms, and she wrapped her arms around his neck. ''I'll always carry you,'' he said. ''You just have to let me.''

Would he? As he carried her effortlessly up the steps to their bedroom, Lindy wondered— Had he changed? Or could she live without love?

He tucked her into the king-size bed that they'd spent so many passionate nights in. ''Let me get you some water,'' he said. Lindy rested her head back on the pillows and closed her eyes. As she did, Grandpa Joe's conversation from earlier that day slipped back into her thoughts.

''But he told you he'd never love me,'' Lindy had said.

''He did,'' Grandpa Joe said. ''But I think he's done some soul-searching since that moment. I think even before he knew about your accident he'd been thinking. Maybe he's changed.''

''Can Shane change? Is that possible?'' she'd asked.

''I don't know,'' Grandpa Joe had admitted. ''He's the only one who can answer that.''

Shane returned a few minutes later with a glass of ice water. ''Here you go.''

He handed it to her, and Lindy took a sip. Ever

since they'd removed her IV, she'd had to work on keeping her body hydrated. "Thanks," she said.

"Anytime. Can I get you anything else? Are you hungry?"

"The hospital dinner was fine," Lindy said. "And I did finally eat my Ho Ho's."

Shane smiled, and Lindy reveled in his lopsided grin. She'd always been partial to his smile. It undid her every time. "That you finally did," he said.

Lindy patted the quilt. "Sit for a while?"

Shane sat on the bed next to her. "What's wrong? Are you feeling okay?"

"I don't know," Lindy admitted. "I still ache, but Shane, you said we needed to talk. Is now finally that time?"

He gazed at her for a long moment. "It can be."

"Then let's talk," Lindy said. She placed her hand on his cheek. He'd shaved before picking her up, and his skin was smooth to her touch. Shane turned his head so that he could kiss the inside of her palm. His movement distracted her and she worked to focus. "I want you to be very honest with me."

"Uh-huh." Shane kissed her palm again, the movement sending delightful prickles up her spine.

She shifted. "Shane, I'm serious."

He moved his head away from her hand and turned his gaze on her. "So am I."

She could see that he was. "So talk," she said.

All sorts of emotions crossed Shane's face in an instant. The emotions flashed so fast that Lindy had no time to comprehend them all.

Shane reached forward and took her fingers in his. He laced his hand into hers and placed it to his lips before asking, "Do you love me?"

A thousand and one sensations shot through Lindy as her mental debate started. "I—" she began.

Shane lowered their linked hands and said, "I heard you that night. You told me that you loved me."

"It was after sex," Lindy said. "It doesn't count. People say all sorts of things that they don't mean after sex."

He quickly masked the stricken expression that crossed his face. "So you didn't mean it?"

Lindy knew that this was her chance to back out. To lie. But she'd lied earlier in their relationship and she herself had just asked him to be honest. And look at what her silence about the baby had cost her. No, it was time for her to admit her feelings, to let her words be the truth, no matter what consequences might arise. With her free hand, she rubbed her temples.

"Headache?" Shane asked, his concern evident.

"No." She didn't have a headache. She had a pressure, a risk to take. She took a deep breath and then she let the words spill forth quickly. "I meant every bit of those words I said that night."

He leaned back slightly, studying her face. "Everyone's said you loved me. My father said it. Tina said it. And now you've confirmed it. I've been a pretty big fool, haven't I?"

"You haven't been the fool," Lindy said. "I have. I fell for you a long time ago. I came to work for you, and then I couldn't leave because I'd fallen in love with you. I wanted you in my life, whatever way I could get you. But you're not the fool, Shane. I was. I let my feelings become unhealthy, and I knew I had to leave. That's why I went to Jacobsen. I had to have perspective. You can understand that, can't you? I couldn't be your long-suffering PA pining away for you any longer.''

''I can understand that,'' Shane said.

He lifted her fingers to his lips again. Lindy had the sudden remembrance of how he'd sucked each one of her fingertips until his lips had finally stopped tormenting her and instead crashed down upon hers. She tugged on her hand a bit, but Shane didn't let go. To divert herself from the sensation, she continued to talk.

''So then I found out I was pregnant, and knew I'd be attached to you forever. We've been through that conversation already, but the result was that we ended up married, had hours and days of great lovemaking, and I fell in love with you even further. And then in a moment of weakness, when I thought you were asleep, I told you how I felt.''

There. It was all out there. Every last word. Realizing she was holding her breath, Lindy slowly exhaled.

Shane gazed over their linked hands, hands that were still close to his lips. ''And telling me how you felt is a bad thing because I didn't say it in return, and I didn't love you back.''

Lindy tugged her hand again, but Shane refused to give it to her. ''Well, yes.''

He kissed their linked fingers. ''I admit that your

words freaked me out. Telling someone you love them brings with it all sorts of things like responsibility, trust and faith. I've never deserved you, Lindy. Heck, my grandfather's made that perfectly clear more times than I can count over these past three years. When you told me you loved me, it hit me here.'' He lowered their linked hands and placed them above his heart. ''All of a sudden I realized that I was responsible for you. Not that I wasn't before, but you'd just given me the most precious gift in the world and trusted me to take care of it. You'd given me your heart. And that frightened me.''

''I know,'' Lindy said. ''You've never loved me, Shane. You've always been in love with a dream, with the image of some girl's hand on the back of a bus representing the tragedy of unrequited love. It's the romantic in you.''

He shook his head with such a force that it startled her. ''No. It's not a romantic thing. It's a foolish thing. It's a protective mechanism I've used and perfected over the years so that I didn't get hurt, so that I let no one hurt me. I dated women, let them use me. And I admit, I used them right back and sent them trinkets at the end.''

''Expensive trinkets.''

''Perhaps. But every woman knew what the relationship was not going to be before she and I ventured into it. Sure, it made me look like a playboy because I seemed to go through women so fast, but I subconsciously found women that I knew I'd never want in my life on a permanent basis. They served one purpose. To prove to myself that I didn't have to risk my heart. These women proved that I didn't have to be alone, that I *chose* to be alone.''

Shane paused. ''I hate talking about past relationships.''

''I was there through many of them,'' Lindy reminded him.

He looked at her earnestly. ''I know. So you know that I wasn't a male slut.''

''I know,'' Lindy said.

''Good. That's important to me. You walked into my life, and suddenly you became important to me. Those women, they weren't. Maybe I did break hearts along the way, but their hearts weren't really interested in making my heart happy. Their hearts broke at losing access to my bank account or to the status that being with Shane Jacobsen affords. Maybe that's why I clung to that memory. That girl at camp only wanted me for me, and there have been very few women who have wanted me for just myself.''

''I did.''

Shane nodded. ''I know. But by the time you came into my life, I was so jaded. I didn't need a PA, but there you were and I wanted you. But not like any of those other women. I didn't want to date you. Somehow I didn't want to tar you with that brush. I wanted you for more than just a few weeks of mutual using. Does that make sense?''

''Yes,'' Lindy said, for it did. Shane had become her friend. He'd shared with her his innermost thoughts. He'd shared with her his journals. With her, he'd simply been Shane.

"I guess it took some alcohol and pain pills to loosen me up enough to let my subconscious desires surface. I don't think I let you go that night."

"No. You called me the love of your life and got me drunk," Lindy said. He arched a blond eyebrow at her, and Lindy grinned as the moment lightened. "Okay, you gave me the first strawberry daiquiri. I'll admit I walked to the bar myself a few times after that."

He acknowledged her confession with a slight nod of his head. "Deep down you've always been the love of my life. That's the conversation Grandpa Joe and I had, the part you didn't overhear. He told me that love isn't a feeling as much as it is a choice. I realized that I am the one that chooses to let the feelings in, to let my feelings flow. I'm the one that chooses to care. He even asked me why I thought I couldn't love you."

Shane stopped to kiss her fingers again, almost as if reassuring himself she was real. "You see, I thought I was a man who couldn't love. But I can love, Lindy. I'd just turned off those emotions. So when I first thought of loving you, I realized that I loved you like a best friend, and then later as the mother of my child. I even thought that I loved you just like I'd love a member of my family. So yes, I'd answered Grandpa Joe's question. But that's not enough, is it?"

He'd mentioned all the ways to love her but the main one. Lindy shook her head. "It's settling. It's being satisfied with less."

"I know. So I asked Harry how he'd known Megan was the one for him. He told me that she was all he thought about. That's when I realized the truth."

A small, wary prickle ran up Lindy's spine. Shane still held her hand. Did she dare to hope? Did she dare to believe? Had Shane—to use a cliché—finally seen the light? He seemed to be waiting for her. "Tell me the truth you learned," she said.

"I learned that you already had the power to hurt me."

Her protest was immediate. "But I never would—"

His free hand reached forward and he placed a forefinger on her lips, silencing her. "I know you would never intentionally hurt me. But the truth is that I'd let you have that power just because I cared about you. Unlike all the others, I needed you. That's why I denied how I felt so much. You had power over me, and to admit my true feelings would give you more. The paradox is that you'd become such a part of my life that I never wanted to let you go, or for our relationship to change."

He smiled at her, a smile that warmed Lindy's heart to its very core. "After I really did some introspection, I realized that's why I'd panicked when you were ill. That's why I'd brought you food after my mother paid you a visit. I cared about you, and I cared deeply. And if I had the courage to admit it to myself, I loved you. Love was why I didn't want you to go to Jacobsen. I didn't want you to leave me because deep down, Lindy, I can't live without you. You're like a half of me that I've always needed, even when I didn't believe it existed.''

"You love me." Hope started to dance inside Lindy, but doubt tempered it. ''But this relationship, me, I'm nothing like you ever expected. I'm nothing that you thought you wanted.''

"Lindy, I was sitting there in my office, after you overheard me. I knew I had to think, to know the truth about myself before I saw you again. That's why I didn't rush right after you. While I sat there, I tried to conjure up the image of that girl on the bus, and do you know what? I couldn't see her face. What I did see, though, was that living without you is the scariest thought in the world. Lindy, when I think of the word love, the only image I see is yours.''

She opened her mouth to speak, but again his finger touched her lip, indicating that he had more to say. ''When I realized that, I knew right then that I had to tell you. So I left the office, and found you. Well, I found your car. The ambulance had already left the scene. That moment began what has probably been the worst nightmare of my life to this point. I loved you, I hurt you, and I didn't know if you were even okay or ever would be okay again.''

"Oh, Shane." Lindy covered their linked hands with her free one, and he followed suit until all their hands touched. ''I'm so sorry.''

His blue eyes glistened. ''No, I am. I'm sorry for not believing. I'm sorry for hurting you. I don't know how I'll ever make it up to you. You heard me say some terrible things to my grandfather, things that I never meant for you to hear.''

''The words did hurt, but your not saying the words I wanted to hear, that hurt, too. It was hard knowing that I loved you, and that you would never love me back. One-sided love is never enough.''

He leaned toward her, closing the gap between them. ''Forgive me, Lindy. I promise it will never be one-sided again. Never again. I love you, and I'm not going to hurt you ever.''

''Shane, we love each other. We'll argue. We'll disagree. We'll sometimes hurt each other with words or actions that deep down we don't mean. Sometimes we'll hurt each other unintentionally. But Shane, we love each other. That means that I trust you to hold my heart and cherish it. That means you'll trust me to do the same. I promise not to let you down, even when sometimes we both make mistakes. That's love, Shane. That's the kind of love that endures.''

''I love you,'' he said.

''And I believe you, my darling.''

Lindy felt her eyes brim with tears. Using a gentle touch, for several quiet moments Shane did nothing but sweep Lindy's tears away. Then he kissed her lips. The kiss he bestowed was tender and sweet, and Lindy returned his kiss with equal gentleness. Even though Shane had kissed her like this before, this time was different.

This kiss held endless promise of a lifetime full of love. This kiss signified the start of the next phase of their relationship. This kiss was their new beginning.

"You know I want you," he whispered against her cheek.

"I want you too," Lindy said, for she did. She wished her body was completely healed so that she could make love to him, and feel him joined together with her.

"Know that," Shane said. "Always know I want you, and not just because we have great sex. Yes, I'd love to bury myself deep inside you and show you how much, but I love you, Lindy, and it's not just about sex. I want you in my life, forever and ever. I love you, Lindy, and I'll spend the rest of my life proving it. That's a promise I plan to keep."

Happiness and peace filled Lindy, and she encircled him in her arms, holding him close. This was her man, and she was his woman. They had been made for each other, and although the path had been rough, they'd discovered that true love did exist.

Shane loved her, truly loved her, and now her world was complete. Gone was the past, and in its place was simply a future that she and Shane would create together.

As his lips lowered down to hers, Lindy knew that she'd never take him for granted. She'd been blessed with a gift in this special man, and she'd spend the rest of her life finding out just how lucky she was. She loved him, and he loved her right back.

Epilogue

Bradley Joseph Jacobsen made his debut early New Year's Day, and slept peacefully through the christening ceremony his Grandfather Blake performed four weeks later.

Grandpa Joe beamed at the great-grandbaby he was holding in his arms. He'd always teased his wife Henrietta that all babies, except theirs of course, were ugly, but he wouldn't even venture to make teasing remarks about Bradley. Bradley had something about him that made him special. Perhaps it was the fact that he bore the proud heritage of the Jacobsen surname. Perhaps it was the security of knowing how much his parents loved him. For when Shane had realized that he loved Lindy, and how much he loved her, he had loved with abandon. No one who came in contact with him could ever doubt how much he loved his wife, and how much she loved him in return. Lindy had completely healed from the accident long before Bradley's arrival, and she'd delivered him naturally with only an epidural for pain support. Shane had been by her side throughout, and had been the one to cut Bradley's cord and hand the infant to his mother, who was waiting impatiently to see the life she'd carried.

"Okay, everyone, smile." The photographer snapped the photo of the four generations: Joe, Blake, Shane and Bradley. Grandpa Joe smiled as he placed the baby back into Lindy's outstretched arms. The photographer now set about organizing Blake's brood, motioning Claire, Nick, Bethany and Olivia into place next to Shane, Lindy and their son.

Since there was still time before the reception, the rest of Grandpa Joe's family milled around the church. The older man felt immeasurable pride as his eyes swept over his clan.

It had been a double christening, Megan and Harry's baby girl, being a little overdue, had been born just two weeks before Bradley. Darci and Cameron had flown in from New York for the ceremony, and had immediately announced they were expecting in late August.

"You look pretty proud of yourself," Andrew said as he approached Grandpa Joe.

"I am," Grandpa Joe replied.

"So, who's next?"

Grandpa Joe feigned innocence. "What do you mean?"

Andrew grinned. "If I know you, you already have something up your sleeve. You've got Claire, Nick and Olivia to marry off. Who's next?"

Grandpa Joe's gaze swept over his grandchildren. Nick was still oblivious to women in general, and Claire was still too busy with work. He already knew their perfect mates, but it would take a little while to put everything in place before he could set those wheels in motion. He rested his gaze on Olivia, and as her Jacobsen blues caught his, she smiled.

Still, years of observing people told Grandpa Joe that something was amiss. Olivia had turned thirty in September, and unlike her twin Nick who couldn't care less, or her older sister Claire who was too busy with her career to even think about her age, Grandpa Joe knew that hitting thirty bothered Olivia.

But for once he was out of ideas. Although he knew some would come to him. Matchmaking ideas always did.

"So who's next?" Andrew repeated as the little gathering finished with the pictures.

Grandpa Joe arched his eyebrows, turned on a devious yet dazzling smile and looked at Andrew. "Wouldn't you like to know," he said. "Just wouldn't you like to know."

HARLEQUIN®

AMERICAN *Romance*®

proudly presents a captivating new
miniseries by bestselling author

Cathy Gillen Thacker

THE BRIDES OF
HOLLY SPRINGS

Weddings are serious business in the picturesque town of
Holly Springs! The sumptuous Wedding Inn—the only place
to go for the splashiest nuptials in this neck of the woods—
is owned and operated by matriarch Helen Hart. This no-
nonsense Steel Magnolia has also single-handedly raised
five studly sons and one feisty daughter, so now all that's
left is whipping up weddings for her beloved offspring....

Don't miss the first four installments:

THE VIRGIN'S SECRET MARRIAGE
December 2003

THE SECRET WEDDING WISH
April 2004

THE SECRET SEDUCTION
June 2004

PLAIN JANE'S SECRET LIFE
August 2004

Available at your favorite retail outlet.

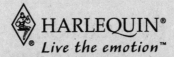

HARLEQUIN®
Live the emotion™

Visit us at www.eHarlequin.com

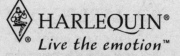

If you enjoyed what you just read,
then we've got an offer you can't resist!

Take 2 bestselling love stories FREE!

Plus get a FREE surprise gift!

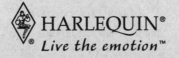

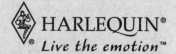

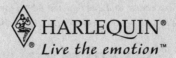

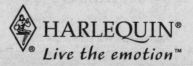